NAMRATA VERGHESE graduated from Emory University in 2019 as a Robert W. Woodruff Scholar. A 'juvenile immigrant' herself, she was born in India and spent her early years in England before moving to the United States. Her writing has appeared in *Tin House Online, Nimrod International Journal of Prose and Poetry, World Literature Today* and elsewhere. *The Juvenile Immigrant* is her first book.

THE JUVENILE IMMIGRANT

Indian Stories from America

NAMRATA VERGHESE

SPEAKING
TIGER

SPEAKING TIGER PUBLISHING PVT. LTD
4381/4, Ansari Road, Daryaganj
New Delhi 110002

Copyright © Namrata Verghese 2019

First published in India by Speaking Tiger in hardback 2019

ISBN: 978-93-89231-11-3
eISBN: 978-93-89231-10-6

10 9 8 7 6 5 4 3 2 1

To Appachan, still the best storyteller I know, and my parents—my first readers, editors and cheerleaders. This book would not exist without you.

Contents

Alone   9

Monsoon   21

#SareeNotSorry   35

The Legal Alien   39

Spellbound   49

Guide to Bharatanatyam   51

Ash   59

Kathakali   61

The Juvenile Immigrant   65

A Love Story in 100 Words   83

Aaja Nachle   85

Enough   93

CONTENTS

Neurons and Hormones   105

Butter Chicken   111

Family History   119

Naale   125

It Dreamt Itself Away   131

Shaadi.com   143

Hyphenated   147

Tara   167

Acknowledgements   171

Alone

The airport security line is a coiling beast of heat and sweat and people in business suits and people in tracksuits, all different degrees of bitter, all different shades of white.

You look down at Anjali, expecting to find her fazed. It's her first international flight, after all. But no, she's so focussed on her game of Candy Crush that she shuffles along mindlessly with the line, zombie feet for a zombie place. Kids these days.

Smiling, you grab her pudgy arm decorated with an array of exactly twelve sparkling bangles from her Bharatanatyam dance class. She doesn't look up, but she lets you hold her, lets you roll your thumb three times over the back of her hand in one direction, then three times in the other. Her wrist relaxes in your fingers.

With your free hand, you haul the roll-on and Anjali's purple Dora backpack onto the baggage screener, your movements practiced and mechanical. You've been a tourist in your own country too many damn times to be bad at it. India, the motherland. The land of your mother, and her constant comments about your weight, your job, your love life or lack thereof. Shaking your head, you remind yourself that there are still thousands of miles and twenty-two hours between the two of you, so you focus on now instead.

Anjali is struggling with her shoes. She insists on wearing laces, even though the ties are difficult for her, just like she insists on being called Angie at school.

'It's cool, Mom,' she told you. 'Mandy says the name Angie is cool, cool, cool.'

Who are you to argue with Mandy?

So you crouch down and help tug her neon-pink sneakers off her feet, socks sagging, laces unravelling. Ten little piggy toes. When she was younger, Anjali would wear sneakers with shiny red lights, and she would twist her body to follow her heels—laughing, laughing, laughing. At ten, she's too old for that, too cool.

'Hey, Angie,' you whisper to her, right before she's about to go through the metal detector. 'If they want to stop you, or touch you, or ask you questions, let them, okay? Don't make a fuss. I'm right here.' It's hard to explain racial profiling to a ten-year-old, so you tell her just what she needs to know.

Anjali's brown eyes are wide, but she doesn't say anything. Her silence is unsettling. She's been quiet a lot lately, so immersed in her pixels and buttons that she fades a little from the real world.

You stand back up, brushing off your jeans and pressing a quick kiss into Anjali's curls. People are giving you strange looks, but you're used to that by now. You've been getting them all your life.

Anjali walks stiffly and cautiously up to the metal detector, flinching only a little. She makes it through, trembling but intact, and you're so proud you feel a tightness in your chest. Standing in line, you pull a funny face at her, and although she doesn't pull one back like she used to do, she still smiles a little bit. And that's enough, for now.

A ham-coloured man with an unsteady mustache comes behind you and tentatively taps you on the shoulder. 'Excuse me, ma'am,' he says, his voice drooping like his facial hair. 'It's your turn.' As if you didn't know already. As if you don't understand how queues work. He says this as though he wants to be harsher, but is wary of upsetting the potential terrorist. Brown skin comes with its occasional perks.

As you're walking through the metal detector, you know the TSA agent will approach you before she actually does. She's exactly the sort to randomly select you, tired and irritated and cynical, with skin still pockmarked from childhood acne and pustules of fat swelling under her jacket.

'I need to pat you down, ma'am,' she says. 'Please come with me to a private room.' She turns sluggishly, and you have no choice but to follow her. Looking back, you see Anjali, sitting on a metal bench the same texture as a cheese grater. She's anxiously chewing on the white string dangling from her hoodie, gnawing methodically, feet swinging just a little bit off the ground. You wave to her, make an apologetic face, and hold up one finger. *One minute. I'll be back in one minute.* She knows what to do, she's a smart girl. She nods. She waits.

The agent leads you to a curtained-off area, and you spread your arms out, feet apart. She squeezes your shoulders, your chest, pats down your legs and your ankles, awkwardly dances around your groin.

The last time someone touched you there was three months ago. In the dark, you could barely make out his features, but his fat jiggled on top of you with every movement, skin against skin in the worst way possible. It was awkward, unpleasant, but somehow still over too quickly. Anjali had accidentally run into him the next morning when she was supposed to be asleep, when he'd been eating her Cheerios from her bowl in her seat.

'No, no, no,' she'd said, running to you and burying her face in your stomach. 'No, no, no,' over and over again, until you asked him to get out, until you told him to call you on the fake number you'd given him and said that it would be great to catch up sometime.

God, he was a bad fuck. Ethan, you think his name was. Still, you can't help but feel grateful for the men who want you, although you make sure you hate yourself for it.

Mark—the genius, the ex-husband, the asshole—was good in bed. An awful man, but good in bed. Back then, it was hard to see past that. That and his crooned words of love that tasted

12

too often of beer, and his spontaneous kisses that made you feel feminine, and his collarbones—so sharp and expressive in a way his words weren't—emerging prominently every time their owner shrugged or grinned, with shadows and hollows and light all featured equally and unselfishly.

You should have listened to your mother when she told you he was bad news. Not because he was white, like she said. Not because he was Christian, like she said. Because he was a chai tea man. A man who would order, 'One chai tea, please and thank you,' with a smug look that only the happily ignorant can wear with impunity.

And because he left you for a blonde, left you because she was blonde, left you pregnant and alone and jobless and scared. Of course, he never admitted this was the reason. What really shocks you isn't that he had the audacity to accuse you of being insane in a thinly-veiled attempt to gain custody of Anjali, but how many people he managed to convince—even your friend and confidante, Dr Banerjee, who was supposed to be on your side. But, you remind yourself, they don't call him a genius for nothing.

The agent finishes her pat-down. She pulls off her gloves, relieved now that she's not touching you, the contaminated object, the young Indian woman who, if American media is to be believed, must be working for Al Qaeda. She hasn't found anything. They never find anything. The bomb is inside you, after all.

'You're good to go, miss,' she says dully, in the same bland tone that Anjali uses when she's upset or tired. 'Have a safe flight.'

'You too,' you say without thinking, and before she can realize your mistake, you hurry away, your dark skin trying hard to blush.

You start towards the bench, wondering how you're going to spin the pat-down to Anjali. 'It's so ticklish,' you imagine telling her. 'They tickle you everywhere, like this!' Her face will break out in a huge grin as she anticipates the 'tickle attack,' and she will laugh and gasp and cry out for you to stop, looking like a child again.

But when you get there, she's gone. Her backpack, her little Dora shoes, everything. Gone.

Your head gets hot, heavy and blank. It's buzzing with everything but comprehension. Buzzing, buzzing, always the buzzing, like when you miss the last stair or pat your pocket and can't feel your phone. Your breath congeals uncomfortably in your chest, but you're not panicking. You're not panicking. Heartbeat echoing loudly around your ears, you walk—*walk, not run, walk, not run*—towards the baggage scanner, willing your feet to move in small, quick steps—*don't trip, don't fall, don't trip, don't fall*. She's not there. She's supposed to be there. She's not there.

You breathe in huffs of three. *One, two, three...one, two, three.* It's an old trick you taught Anjali to calm her down. It never worked with her.

'Excuse me,' you say to one woman, a tired-looking mother

with creases pulling her eyes down her cheeks. Your voice is barely audible. She looks at you with mild concern, but you shake your head quickly, hot tears jabbing your eyes.

Gulping down thick chunks of saliva, you practice, like you do at the Starbucks drive-thru, like you used to before your teacher took roll in class. *Excuse me, have you seen a ten-year-old girl? She's Indian, and she is wearing a pink sweater and jeans.* Words become meaningless when they're said over and over again. Words become precious when there's still so much left to say.

'My daughter,' you finally blurt out to the woman, who by now looks as though she would do anything to be away from you. 'I can't...' *—swallow, clench your throat, what do you normally do with your tongue?*—'I can't find my daughter.' You're whispering, but she hears. Or understands, somehow.

'Oh my god,' she says, one of her hands instinctively reaching for her own toddler, the other grasping your shoulder. 'Oh my god, okay, it's going to be okay. Hold on. Stay here. No, come with me. I'll get help.'

Turning around with maternal alacrity, she yells out to the nearest uniformed official, 'Sir! Please come here! This lady's daughter is missing!'

The TSA agent's eyes snap up from the computer, and you can almost imagine his panic. *This is what I was trained for.*

He murmurs unintelligible words into his neck as he approaches you, and his cologne surrounds you, wafting fairy dust in the air. Where is Anjali you ask and he says we're going to find her ma'am, we're on it right now, don't you worry.

You're sitting down, there are hands on your shoulders, they're not yours but their warmth helps. You're saying, '4'3, 72 pounds, pink, pink, pink.' They keep asking, but they don't understand, her description isn't going to change. She is. Find her. Find her.

A woman gives you a bottle of water to sip, to 'calm your nerves,' as if nerves are your problem. Dasani. Fancy tap water. Anjali would only drink Fiji. It's the same agent who gave you a pat down long ago, so long ago. Was that today? The water tastes like bile, but you swallow it anyway, gulp, your throat is working, you're doing something, you're alive.

'Can I look for her?' you ask, like you've already asked, you continue to ask, you will keep asking.

No, it's a safety hazard. Just stay calm. We'll find her, she can't have gotten far.

You don't understand, she's not like normal kids. She's different. People will hurt her.

We understand, ma'am. Please try to remain calm. We will find her. Could you describe her for us one more time?

4'3, 72 pounds, pink pink pink pink pink pink pink. Blink on, blink off, memorize your script and recite it like an understudy-turned-lead. How long have you been dead?

The airport is a hospital; you taste blood on your tongue. Your nose is raw; your breathing, brittle. Blink on, blink off. Swallow convulsively. Tend to your wind-chime bones. You presume you came from somewhere, but this is all you get, in a dream: the noise of lethargic travellers, the fading of befores, the absence of afters.

The brightness becomes dark, the darkness lights up with a blue and red pulse. A heartbeat. *An. Ja. Li.* The place is a riddle, vacant space organized into a puzzle. Your answer has already been imagined and forgotten. *Where are you?*

You look up. It's been a while, maybe minutes, maybe hours. Her father should know. It's the right thing to do. You're trembling. You hold your phone up in fascination, watching as it vibrates under your fingers. You hate that you remember his number by heart. You hate that you can't forget.

Groups of three. 428 871 946. That last digit, Anjali hates it so much. Why is there always one left over? 9. She eats Cheerios like that too, in trios, packs, each one a clique that smirks at the outsiders. *You can't sit with us.* She cries if there is one left over.

It's ringing. You know he won't hang up, not this time, because you've changed your number since you last called him and you don't ask him for child support anymore. He's a writer, a genius, he won't be able to hang up on an unknown number. He'll be too curious. Stories are everywhere. You should know, you used to write his for him.

'Hello?'

His voice is so horrifyingly familiar. After all these years. The tears come back, they always come back. You wait for them to change you but they never do. You can't stop crying.

You sound crazy, you know you sound crazy. He always called you crazy.

'Mark,' you finally say, and there's silence. Static crackles on the line. 'Mark, our daughter is missing.' And your words are steady for once, they are whole and round and despite everything, you are proud of this. It's like you're equals here, now, finally.

'Fuck,' you hear him swear quietly, and for a second, you're glad he cares, but then—'I told you not to call this number, didn't I? God, what the fuck'—and then there's a beep and he's gone.

'Mark,' you say to the dead line. Mark, mark, mark, *mark my words mark*, that's something you've always wanted to say to him and now you can't and you never will. *Mark, mark my words.*

The TSA agent is back and something is different. Shoulders back, spine straight, mouth set. What happened?

You can't say anything, but your mouth opens and closes, opens and closes, you are a fish gasping at hollows in a frozen lake. *Anjali?*

What is that expression on the agent's face? The expression that used to be pity but is now something else, something that you can't identify but still recognize.

'Ma'am,' she says, and she doesn't sit down with you, not this time, she stands apart, twenty feet apart probably, although you have no way of knowing this. Feet shoulder width apart. Power stance. This, you know.

'Ma'am, you said your daughter is a ten-year-old child, around four feet tall, wearing a pink jacket, correct?'

Yes yes yes. 4'3, 72 pounds, pink pink pink pink. You nod, up and down, up and down.

She takes a step back now. 'Ma'am, I'm sorry, but I think there's been a misunderstanding.'

Why is she backing away? What misunderstanding? *Where are you?*

'We've gone over the security footage, and, well…' she reaches up, rubs the nape of her neck. She's uncomfortable, not authoritative. She won't last long in this job. 'Well, there's no one there, ma'am. We matched up the times from when you entered the airport to when you entered the security line.'

Eyes dart away. Blank stares. Blink on, blink off. 'Do you understand, ma'am? There was no child with you. You were alone.'

Alone. Linguistically, that's [ə'ləʊn]. But knowing that doesn't help you right now.

You look at her and you are still. Her mouth is moving, but it's just noise, no words. You keep quiet. Your skin doesn't fit quite right. The buzzing. The buzzing.

She gives you a puzzled look, pity coming back. You recognize that, you know pity, but she leaves slowly, muttering something to the staff member on her way out about not letting you leave.

The buzzing, the buzzing, it's coming from your phone.

There's a call. It's Mark, it's got to be Mark, you knew he cared, he is a genius after all—

Damn it. The screen glows bright in the darkness, an intricate spiral of white light spelling out *Dr Banerjee.* That stupid fucking shrink, didn't you fire him last week?

Irritated, you jab the red button as hard as you can, so hard a bubble forms around your finger and ripples across the touchscreen. The incessant buzzing stops.

Stillness. The world is quiet now.

Where are you?

Monsoon

The Wet Season
Chengannur, India, 2003

We move to England when I am four years old. On our last evening at home, my grandfather and I sit outside on the verandah together, eating cold skewers of mango and exchanging stories. He rocks slowly in a bamboo chair; I curl by his knees, back pressed against iron railings. I listen as the Pandavas battle their enemies, swords slicing stomachs, winning wars. I close my eyes and imagine Draupadi in front of me, her sari unravelling into infinity. I don't want to open my eyes. I don't want the stories to end, because we are leaving tomorrow, and I will not hear them again. Some part of me knows this.

'Tell me one more,' I ask my grandfather, more plea than request.

He smiles. 'Last one.' An old book of photos lies open by our feet, its mildewed pages curling in the humidity. He points to the picture I've been fixated on: my grandmother before she became my grandmother. Sepia. Still. Neck heavy with marigold, blush blurring into sari. The caption at the bottom of the peeling photo reads: *Wedding Portrait, 1968.*

The marriage had been the event of the year, my grandfather tells me. Guests travelled from the farthest reaches of the peninsula—Madras, Mangalore, some even from such faraway lands as Madhya Pradesh. My grandmother couldn't pick her groom, so she focussed on her sari, designing it with gold thread from Lahore, tiny diamonds from Delhi. The night before her wedding, she lay awake and wondered if her husband would be tall or round or thin or kind.

My grandfather doesn't know whether he lived up to her expectations, he says, but he did the best he could. When they moved into their first home together, he cleared an acre in the back for her to cultivate a garden, a hobby she'd mentioned to him just once before. The only tree that survived their first foray into gardening was the mango tree—the tree next to us now, its lowest branches tickling and tangling in my hair. Every year, my grandparents would usher in the monsoon by eating the fruit together, sitting on the verandah late into the night, their chins sticky with juice.

Years after my grandmother's death, my grandfather continues the ritual. Although my grandmother had been the gardener, he picked up the hobby in her absence. He filled her emptiness with roots. Since that first monsoon, their garden has flourished, every inch alive and growing. Jackfruit trees, tapioca plants, coconut palms heavy with hairy shells. My grandfather's palms became calloused, his fingernails permanently crusted with dirt. Even among the abundance, my grandfather's favourite spot in the garden is the small patch of earth where he and my grandmother first planted that tiny mango sapling. At the time, it was just a bright sliver of green, labouring for the sky. Now, it towers over the other trees. When he plucks that first fruit of the season, my grandfather says, he feels, for a moment, like he is not alone. When he tastes mangoes, he knows he's home.

The story complete, my grandfather falls quiet, a faraway look in his eyes. We sit out there, my grandfather and I, until white light melts into gold, until crickets start chirping in the rain-soggy air. I rest my head on his knees and watch the sun die. My childhood: Crayola skies and humid nights.

My grandfather startles the silence only once—to ask me if I will remember these stories. His stories. Yes, Appachan, I promise, nodding my head up and down with vigour. Yes, I will. I squint at the last piece of mango left on my plate: the core, the part we usually cut out and throw away. This time, I slurp it like a lollipop, committing the taste to memory. The taste of mangoes. The taste of home.

The Dry Season
Manchester, England, 2003

The trip to England is blurry, hot and tear-soaked. I beg my grandfather not to let me go. While my parents load luggage into a taxi, I climb up a pillar of our home, hugging it tightly, refusing to move. My grandfather laughs at my stubbornness. Only he can manage to talk me down, with a few choice words and a smoky embrace—although he gave up cigarettes years ago, my grandfather has always smelled slightly of smoke and earth. His tone is glib—silly girl, he says, why stay at home when you can go on an *adventure*? You need to go, so that you can one day tell *me* stories—but his last hug is shaky.

Even after our plane lands on British soil, I hold the memories in my mind, just as my grandfather instructed. I study them the way I will study flash cards before a test, running over their small details when I try, futilely, to sleep in my new home. I remember, because I have promised to, the crickets, the sunsets, the ripples of heat that approach and retract. The monsoon sky turning a colour not quite blue and not quite grey.

By now, something has changed in my mother. She doesn't tell me, but I can tell, the way children can. A thrumming of insect wings, a pulse kick-starting to life. Her stomach stretches and dimples, zigzagged with red veins, a pouch of warm soil for seeds to take root.

My sister is born eight months after we move. Her first word is 'Mummy,' not 'Amma'. As she grows, she speaks with the crisp, clipped tones of a British child—the accent that I could never quite master. Words tumble out of her mouth, angled and clanging, and I strain my ears to understand. I begin to fear the day she will grow up and recognize her superiority over me. I realize it has started already when, one night, she scolds my father for scooping rice into his mouth with his hands instead of a fork. When I blush because she makes her Ken kiss my Barbie, she deems me a prude. Her childhood: plastic dolls and costume tiaras.

Houston, Texas, 2007

My third-grade homeroom teacher stumbles over my name on my first day of American school. 'Nam—uh—'

The stutter is as familiar to me as my own name. Per my conditioning, I raise my hand.

'Dude, that's so cool.' The girl next to me points to the henna designs winding up my fingers, her words sticky with slimy pink gum. 'Your parents let you get a tattoo?'

I am the only Indian enrolled in my expensive private school. By now, we have moved for the third and last time—from England to Houston, Texas. The day before, a new friend from church had brought over a fat tube of henna paste. In celebration of the imminent first day of school, we gleefully etched designs on each other's hands, painstakingly following stencil patterns of peacocks, flowers, suns. The pungent burnt orange swirls smell like India.

'It's not a tattoo, Grace,' comes the response from the back of the classroom, before I can so much as process Grace's words. 'Don't you know Indians draw those things on? My mom says it's because they worship the devil. Savages.'

The class explodes into snickers; even the teacher's mouth twitches.

The girl laughs too, a sharp, hard sound. 'I've seen a picture of your gods. One of them's a monkey. Your people are so stupid. No wonder you can't even talk English properly!'

That night, I will go home and begin my project. Over the next few years, I will watch hours of American TV, practising and perfecting the slurred words: the hardened, flattened t's and r's, the short syllables and the bored drawl. I will iron my coarse curls, breaking them until they are straight and limp, replacing my oil-slick plaits with the popular layered look of the day. I will flirt with boys and gossip with girls. I will carve myself from the inside out, bleeding, blurring the lines between reality and pretence.

But I have not yet learned the game. Today, in this moment, I have no response. I fend off tears and attempt to laugh along. Later, on the playground, a group of girls are braiding hair in a line. I don't dare approach them. Instead, I watch from the swing-set. The mean girl from class scowls when she sees me and storms over, half her hair braided, the other half swinging loose and straight and shining. 'What do you want?' she demands. 'Go back home! Get out of my country, savage.'

Houston, Texas, 2016

Get out of my country. The first time my brother hears the phrase, he is only eight years old. I had, naively, assumed my brother was safer than me, that the world had changed since I ran, crying, from the playground during my first ever recess in an American school. I am proven wrong on November 9, 2016, the day after a watershed presidential election. That morning, my brother wins the first prize in his science fair. That afternoon, he stumbles out of the school bus, shaking. The second-place winner had told him he was a liar, a cheater. He had told him to go home, or Trump would make him.

'Home?' my brother asks my father that night. 'Isn't this my home?' My brother is the only one of our family born in America, the only one with the right to call this home. Still, my father cannot bring himself to answer the question.

Olathe, Kansas, 2017

'Get out of my country.'

Lying in bed, scrolling through my newsfeed, I learn that

these may have been the last words Srinivas Kuchibhotla heard.

Kuchibhotla and a friend, Alok Madasani, were unwinding, watching a basketball game in a bar after a long workday, when a man entered the bar. Described as 'agitated' by witnesses, the man immediately began hurling racial slurs at the two Indians, dubbing them 'terrorists' and demanding to know their 'legal status'. Moments later, he opened fire. Srinivas Kuchibhotla was killed on the spot; Alok Madasani suffered severe injuries. A third man who intervened to help, Ian Grillot, was wounded in the cross-fire.

The murderer did not attempt to cover up his crime. Instead, he was caught because he bragged, loudly, publicly, about 'killing two Middle Eastern men.'

Chengannur, India, 2017

We visit India for the first time in five years the summer before I start college. The flight is cool, dry. Itchy. I spend it watching Hindi movies starring actresses that look like white, beautiful versions of what I could be. From my window, I can see the Statue of Liberty, and privately—not publicly, never publicly, because I am not a terrorist—I can think that she is not as impressive as people make her out to be.

We land, and I anticipate a homecoming. But when my family meets us in India, they look at me and I know they are surprised, because they expected me to be beautiful. I am American, after all. I should have straight, shiny brown-black hair all the way down my back; my skin should glow white in the suffocating sun, like in the movies from the airplane. But I don't, it doesn't, and they're mystified. What's the point of going to America, then?

My cousins dress the way they think I would be dressed. Bell-bottom jeans, fake Hollister shirts. Bright hellos perfected by years of studying American sitcoms. I stutter a greeting to them, using words I have not tasted in so long, words that glue themselves to my tongue like peanut butter. My inflections aren't right, but they stifle their giggles.

We are all trying. We are all trying so hard.

Later that week, we learn that my grandfather has dementia. Alzheimer's. It isn't too bad yet, sometimes he misplaces his keys. One night, he wandered away from home in search of something. He couldn't remember what. Over the two years that follow, I will hear my stoic father sobbing over the phone, introducing himself to his father over and over again.

It is on this visit that I am forced to recognize that India is not *home* anymore. I am a tourist in my home country. My clothes are wrong, my hair is wrong. I am wrong. My Malayalam is accented, broken. My mother tongue has become a foreign language.

I envy the Facebook friends who splatter their India trips all over my newsfeed. They 'find themselves' in my birthplace. They wear harem pants and wind silk dupattas around their heads. They write about the people they meet, who live bravely in poverty, who treat their visitors like royalty despite their differences. They claim India in a way I have never been able to.

Colour is visible. Colour is visceral. The most primitive taxonomy. I am supposed to be honest. I am supposed to speak up, tell the truth, tell my truth. This becomes difficult to do when, clinging to the culture that is mine and not mine, I feel like a fraud.

Atlanta, Georgia, 2017

In college, I learn the words. I wield them proudly and desperately, this long-awaited lexicon that promises to explain, to help. To heal. *Microaggression. Hegemony. Discrimination. Gaslighting. Trauma.*

Trauma, I learn, is typically conceived of as a rupture, a shattering. I have attempted, many times, to trace my trauma to its root, to find that first rupture. Was it the moment my family boarded a plane bound for England? Or the moment my brother was born an American? Perhaps it was the day English ships first docked on the Kerala coast, four hundred years ago. Perhaps it was the day they left, eighty years ago.

Or perhaps it was all of these things and none of them. Perhaps trauma can be many tiny ruptures, many small shatterings. Abrasions that we accrue, slowly and subconsciously, until our whole bodies are red and raw and scabbing.

Maybe I am scraped, just a little, just enough to sting but not bleed, every time I look at my Texas driver's license—vertical, not horizontal, a marker of difference—or any official government-issued document, embossed with the words, 'Residency Status: Legal Alien.' Every time I make up a fake name at Starbucks so I don't hold up the line while my barista asks my name once, then again, louder, then sighs and asks me to spell it for her. Every time an Uber driver greets me with *namaste* when I enter the car, every time he insists on asking me where I'm from—no, not Texas, where I'm *really* from, *originally*. Every time my white yoga teacher plays 'Hindu' music in the background of a mostly-white class. '*Namaste* means I honour the way your body moves,' she says at the beginning of class. She's wrong, of course—her translation exoticizes and sexualizes a commonplace greeting. But my grade in the class depends on her judgment, so I bite my tongue, over and over again. I cut skin; I taste metal.

The Wet Season
Chengannur, India, 2018

This year's monsoon is one of epic proportions. Rivers burst, sand erodes, people drown. My grandfather's Alzheimer's worsens. When we call relatives in India, they speak, in hushed tones, of my grandfather's condition. They encourage us to sort out our visas, to prepare ourselves for the worst sort of homecoming.

'Appacha,' I say to him on the phone one night, the covers yanked over my head, the phone tight like a lifeline in my hand. 'Tell me a story.'

'Not now, mol,' he says. 'I just told you the one about the tailor.'

'Again. Please.' But he's lost, drifting in and out of consciousness. The stories fade from his mind, replaced by a vast nothingness that engulfs names, faces and memories. Sometimes, he remembers me, but only as a four-year-old; sometimes, I am the live-in nurse and he needs more water. In a rare moment of lucidity, he asks me to come home. 'The mangoes are almost ripe,' he says. 'They'll be ready by the time you get here.'

My mouth goes dry. For the last few months, my grandfather has been living with my uncle, his eldest son. The old house had been sold and bulldozed, making room for industrial development that will never materialize.

'Appacha,' I say. 'The mango tree is gone.'

'Sherikkum?' There is only a tinge of curiosity in his tone. 'No matter. We'll plant another one.'

At the beginning of summer that year, my grandfather is bedridden; by the end, he is gone. I know he is dead before my father tells me the news. My stomach tightens as I hear his footsteps on the stairs, distinctly heavy and slower than usual. I am prepared. And then I'm not. We receive our green card just in time for the funeral.

When I visit the old house with my parents afterwards, I find almost nothing left. My father's childhood home lay shattered in front of us, a heap of wood and brick, home to a few stray cats and dogs undoubtedly infected with all sorts of unspeakable diseases.

I sit on the ground, on what used to be our verandah. I pick up the soil of my childhood, rub it between my fingers as those quiet evenings filled with my grandfather's steady voice and the fragrance of mango blossoms wash over me. My hands run over roots, rough and tangled in the earth, and I realize I've unearthed the mango tree. Because I have promised that I will never forget, I remember that my grandfather had said planting the roots of a tree will grow a new one. So I pack the earthy mess in my suitcase, desperate to see his old magic grow in my new home.

The roots get confiscated at customs when we land. An American entry rule: 'No foreign invasive species permitted.'

#SareeNotSorry

I. Cecily

The material, sourced from the most renowned vendors: gold thread from Lahore; silk, an iridescent red, from Andhra Pradesh. Only the best for Thomas saar's daughter. The gold is embroidered in miniscule curlicues, each stitch done by hand. When Kamla, the artisan, pricks her finger while working by candlelight deep into the night, her blood mingles with the dye dubbed 'red madder'.

Cecily twists in front of the mirror, admiring how the light rolls off her sequined backless blouse, complaining that the tight sleeves have left angry red welts on her upper arm. She misses the stain on the pleats that, if seen through squinted eyes, complements the floral embroidery: a single bloody rose.

Cecily sees Roy properly for the first time on the day of their wedding. It is a lavish affair: yellow-white Hyderabadi biryani is piled high in copper pots, garnished with bright green coriander; oily vats of Chicken Chettinad proclaim, proudly, that this is a non-veg, entirely Christian affair. The only other time she met Roy was through demure, lowered lashes, shrouded by the gauzy dupatta her mother had pulled over her head for modesty. Now, she sees that his smiles are quick, his frowns rare, his contours rounded with age. Spectacles, perched on a bump on his nose, lend him a dignified air.

Later that night, she slips out of the sari in a train station bathroom. She folds up the shimmering yards of material in a tight square, and carefully places it into a black overnight duffel. Emerging in a cotton churidar, the remnants of her first life zipped at her side, she is born anew to vendor cries of vada, vada, vadee, vada.

II. Rani

Years later—twenty-four years later, to be exact—the sari is found again. It had sat gathering dust on the back shelf of Cecily's alamari, along with other garments that tell the story of her life: her maternity nighties, Roy's too-small pants, Rani's baptism frock. It is for Rani, now, that Cecily pulls down the sari, and takes the blouse to the tailor to be altered for her daughter's compact frame. During the fitting, Rani whines about the outdated cut of the neck and Cecily can only watch, pained, as the neckline she designed so lovingly is hacked per her daughter's instructions, cut into a heart-shaped mess.

Rani's wedding is a much more modest affair than hers. A love marriage. The boy, Shibu, is a decent, earnest engineer with eyes that twitch irregularly behind foggy glasses. There is just a hint of scandal: although both families are Malayali and Christian, one is better off. While Roy had blustered about this, privately, Cecily admired her daughter's quiet conviction. Rani was always bolder than she was, or maybe she was just more able to be.

Two weeks after the small church wedding, Rani announces that they are moving to America. Shibu has a scholarship to study bioengineering in North Carolina; Rani will tend to the house, and resume working as a teacher when their green card is finalized. Cecily helps her daughter pack, fingering every dupatta and blouse as she folds it.

She doesn't know this yet, but this will be the last time Rani sees Roy alive. After his heart attack a year from now, she will attempt to return home, but will be blocked by USCIS officers who threaten not to let her back into the country if she leaves. Roy will die on the operating table during his bypass surgery. Still resentful of his daughter's marital choice, his last words to her will be a gruff, 'Be safe.'

III. Shreya

Roy doesn't live to meet Shreya, a full, fizzy child with his easy smile and bright eyes. Cecily sees her only in increments of four, when Shreya is zero, four, eight, twelve, and sixteen years old. On this visit, the last Cecily will remember before she succumbs to the dementia that has haunted her family for generations, Shreya finds the wedding sari tucked away. Rani had not taken it with her. She had no use for such ornamental outfits in North Carolina. It lay forgotten until Shreya pulled it down with sticky, eager fingers. 'Can I try it on, Ammachy?' she asks. 'It's so beautiful. Please, please, please?'

The sari is old now. Loose threads and sequins jut out. The famous red madder dye has melted into a deep pink. Cecily hesitates only for a minute before saying yes. Shreya resembles her more than she does Rani; seeing her now, with her full figure and curly hair and red sari, Cecily is reminded eerily of herself as a young bride. She shakes her head vigorously, ridding herself of musty ghosts. Shreya parades around in the sari, refusing to take it off even at dinner, laughing when she spills a brown spoonful of sambar onto its pleats. She makes Cecily take pictures of her from thirty-six different angles, which she then uploads to a Facebook album entitled 'India 2017 <3', accompanied by the hashtag #SareeNotSorry.

The Legal Alien

Every morning, Susamma wakes up to the same absurd anxiety that Shaji is dead. She texts him immediately, her hands groping for the charging phone on her nightstand out of muscle memory.

'Reached safely?' After the 'R', her phone auto-suggests the rest of the phrase to her, too smart for its own good.

Regardless of what her husband is doing at the time, Susamma always receives the same response within the next five minutes: a terse 'yes'. All lower-case.

Although she last saw Shaji only two hours ago—when she rubbed the sleep out of her eyes, put his chaaya in a thermos, and went back to sleep—something inside her uncoils when she reads this. An unwittingly held breath is released. Now, the day can begin.

Susamma's fear is part spousal affection, part survival instinct. If anything happened to Shaji, she—and her children and her dog and her house—would crumble. Not because she was weak, but because she was dependent. Legally. Despite living in the States for over eleven years, Susamma was still suffocated by the H-4 dependent visa that forced unemployment on her. It bound her to Shaji's H1-B work visa in a tie tighter than marriage, loyalty, or love: a legal bond. If—God forbid—anything happened to Shaji before their I-140 green card application was approved, she would have under a month to pack up her life and return to India.

Shaji's leftover chaaya is cold now, but as she ages more, Susamma finds herself caring less. She heats it up in the microwave instead of the stove. She can't remember when she sat down, but finds herself in the armchair facing the garden, the armchair that has grown accustomed to her contours. Absentmindedly, she takes a sip of tea and gags on the film gathered on its tepid surface. When she stands to scoop the scum out, her back clicks in protest. Her weight swings heavily from horizontal to vertical planes. Shaji had always been heavy, even when they first met, but his weight had a certain gravitas to it. Unlike hers. Hers is more of an unfurling—a letting go. She starts to think of how old she is becoming, how she had achieved the seemingly oxymoronic combination of frail and fat, but shakes the thought out of her head. These days, everything reminds her of decay.

If it were a weekend, her routine would have shifted only slightly, shifted to accommodate one more person: Shaji, sitting beside her, most likely, at the sun-room breakfast table. Clacking furiously on his laptop. She hates the way its pixelated glare always casts eerie twin mini-screens onto his glasses. The English language was too harsh for him—too much emotion behind the ink and paper, too many meaningful permutations of the same words. The language that rejected him until he decided to reject it back. His coding languages are simpler, more efficient. More powerful ways of speaking, he likes to explain to her. When he types, his neck curves over and under. Away, in any case. Over the years, she's learned to love this bent neck, and the small pooch of a double-chin revealed only when he types, just as much as his eyes. She always loved his eyes. When he first proposed, they shone deep and brown. Giddy copper pennies. Time has matted their shine into a soft, patient glow, diffused by bright white laptop-light.

Susamma forgets why she came into the kitchen before looking down and seeing the teacup in her hand. Her fingers have grown too thick for its delicate china handle, so she grips its bottom stoutly. She hovers over knives and pots and pans before finding the right sized spoon to scoop out tea scum. The execution of such mundane chores makes her too aware of her hands, swollen with edema and trained for much greater tasks than this.

The phone rings halfway through the tea's resurrection, and Susamma is mildly disappointed by her indifference to its summons. Once, every ringtone would send a thrill through her as she raced upstairs to grab the landline. The identity of the caller was a cherished guessing-game, the reward for which was hours of blessed chatter in uninhibited Malayalam. Now, she knows it has to be either Bindu or spam.

'Hello, Bindu kutty,' she musters, plastering an ambitious smile on her face that she wills her daughter to hear over the phone. 'How are you, mol?'

'Hey, Mom,' comes the reply, and Susamma has to fight the urge to roll her eyes. The roommate must be within earshot. Bindu only puts on her practice-made-perfect American drawl as a performance. 'Nothing, just doing homework. How's everything back home?'

Susamma makes small talk, exclaiming over the new gladioli she planted a few weeks ago, noting that the forecast predicted rain, which would be a good thing for them. She wonders if Bindu ever feels the same anxiety she does, the same fear that grips her heart every day at seven a.m. After all, her daughter is in her first year of college. Before long, she'll be twenty-one and unable to remain a dependent on her father's visa. But Susamma doesn't worry for Bindu, specifically; she's always been a clever girl. She'll marry strategically, or apply for a green card herself. Who knows—she may even get it before her parents do.

Biju—now he was a different story. Bindu's twin and unsuspecting rival, he was the one Susamma truly worried for, with a desperation that wrenched, frequently and abruptly, at her heart.

Biju had been the most beautiful baby. Full, rosy lips and a dark head of curls. While Bindu went home, he spent his early days in the ICU. Even then, he gurgled at her from the crib, clamping hot little fingers around her thumb and refusing to let go. Love, not instinct, she'd told herself. Her miracle child. She would've never known anything was wrong if he had only smiled. Such a simple, easy, immense thing. A smile.

Shaji had been against the diagnosis from the start. Biju was bright, brighter even than Bindu, he pointed out; he just showed it differently. He would immerse himself in memorizing the detailed diet of the long-extinct diplodocus, or the batting statistics of each player on the Indian national cricket team. He wouldn't talk much, just like Shaji when he was young, preferring the company of books or video games. He was absolutely fine, but Susamma's coddling was just making the situation worse.

When Biju was in fourth grade, however, they'd been called in for a sombre parent-teacher conference with Pattie Friedman, a generically pretty woman whose hair fell in a dark-light gradient she had once, in a happier meeting, explained to them as 'ombre'. Her grey eyes were quiet when she told them that Biju had been accused of sexually harassing a girl. Touching her inappropriately.

Susamma's throat went raw. Her baby. Her Biju. It wasn't possible. After they probed deeper, refusing to leave the classroom until Pattie revealed exactly what transpired that day, they found out that the girl had presented Biju with a red heart during their class Valentine's Day party, along with a declaration of love. He, not knowing any better, had harnessed the only knowledge he had about relationships, attempting to do the 'grown-up thing' with her.

He'd been expelled the same day. Blackballed from all the charter schools in the area. As a parting gesture, Pattie had the audacity to squeeze Susamma's upper arm in sympathy, her bird-fingers covering less than half its circumference. 'Listen, Susan,' she'd said, and Susamma could barely hear her over the raging heartbeat thudding in her ears. 'I've spent a lot of time with Biju, and I think it may be worthwhile getting him…well…checked out, if you know what I mean.'

Susamma's smile hid her teeth grinding furiously behind closed lips. 'I understand. Thank you, Patti.' She took secret pleasure in pronouncing the name in as Indian a manner as possible. *Patti*. Malayalam for 'bitch'.

The tests that followed were lengthy. Expensive. Half the time, Susamma felt as though she would also be diagnosed with a disorder, if she had to interact constantly with old white men forcing her to sort Legos by colour and size. In the end, the diagnosis still doesn't fit comfortably in her mouth: 'Asperger's'. Such an American word, an ugly word, a mouth-curving, vomit-emulating word.

The expulsion hadn't seriously hurt Biju, of course, although Susamma wishes she'd known this would be the case back then. It would have saved her a few dozen grey hairs. He is now studying computer science at Caltech. He's matured into a serious, quiet man whose silence is often mistaken for haughtiness, not obliviousness. He never calls home. Susamma makes it a point to call him every Friday, at 6 p.m. his time. If she calls at any other time, he won't pick up.

As soon as Susamma puts the landline down, her cell phone pings. She still marvels at it, sometimes. The world in her hands. Oh, she is getting old.

'Gdmrng,' the Facebook message read. 'Happyfriday.'

Back in medical school, Susamma had been a centre of gravity. After marriage, for a long time, she felt like a moon out of orbit. As though something rightfully hers had been taken away. Here, where no one cared for her or about her, it was easy to be alone. It was harder to be lonely. Shaji, perhaps out of guilt for his anti-social nature that rendered it difficult for Susamma to maintain friendships, had introduced her to Facebook two years ago. Reconnecting with her old circle had been rejuvenating: within a week, she received over six hundred friend requests. There was that old thrum within her once more. But something still felt off, wrong. This time, it was an emptiness borne not of a lack, but a surplus.

So when Ajay messaged her six months ago, she responded.

In his Facebook profile picture, Ajay wore a neon yellow shirt and dark sunglasses. He posed against a palm tree. It had taken Susamma a few hard squints to place him in her memory: Ajay, the scrawny boy one year her senior in college. Pimple-studded, growth-stunted. He had pursued her relentlessly; she hadn't spared him a second glance. But that was then. Now, Facebook told her Ajay was a successful neurosurgeon working in California. He'd never married, but posted pictures with a rotating cast of slim, beautiful blonde women, usually in front of his Mercedes. He'd grown into his face, in a way, with his cheeks fuller and his beard darker. He regularly went on vacations to the Bahamas, to Mexico, to South America—he had his green card. Or better still, his citizenship.

It had been close to six months of daily messaging. Not much more than good morning or good afternoon. Still. At his insistence, once, she'd spoken with him on the phone, to 'catch up', to reminisce about 'old times'. She had plenty of memories of the old times, but none that featured him. Positively, at least. Still.

'Hallo, hallo,' he'd said, as soon as she picked up the phone. 'It's Ajay.' He pronounced his name Ay-Jay, but still spoke thickly and brownly. He had no time for small talk. 'Have you left that kelavan yet?' was his first question.

Susamma laughed, a little too emphatically. 'No, no. And I've no plans to!' She made excuses to hang up on him. She messaged him the next day. Still.

It was frivolous—silly, really—to daydream. To wonder what life would have been like if she'd paid attention to Ajay back then, back when it was an option. To live comfortably—no, extravagantly—in the lap of luxury. To practice the profession she'd worked so hard to master. To wake up and not worry, for once, if her husband is alive.

She's about to respond to Ajay when another phone alert

vibrates her hand. Strange. This was not part of her routine. Her heart slows when she pulls up the notification: an email from the law firm with 'Immigration Update' in the subject line.

Hands shake. Spit congeals in her mouth. A bad taste coats her tongue. She opens the email.

The I-140 application was approved, it reads. *We will send you the approval notice once we get it.*

Mostly, Susamma is stunned by the brevity of the message.

How something so large can be conveyed by something so small.

Author's Note*: The story clearly dates itself to before 2015, when President Obama's executive action allowing employment authorization for spouses of H1B visa holders came into effect. Notably, the H4-EAD—as the employment authorization is called—is now in danger of being revoked as part of the Trump administration's aggressive 'Hire American' policies.*

Spellbound

Win the spelling bee and you will know what it means to be lonely.

'You beat them!' my father says. His dark skin tries hard to flush. But I did not beat *them*; I beat her: Maddy Johnson—blue-eyed, blonde-haired. We are in fifth grade, but our battle is older.

Win the spelling bee and you will know what it means to master the tongue that has mastered you. To boast of your victory in the language of your master. My winning word was *aubergine*: a u b e r g i n e. *Aubergine.*

'I knew you would get it right,' my father tells me during the car ride home, 'because it's a word from Sanskrit.'

I smile. I nod. I did not know this. I do not know Sanskrit; I know: *Sanskrit.* s a n s k r i t. *Sanskrit.*

Guide to Bharatanatyam

Step One: *Tatta Adavu* (Tapping)

Tapping is first. Tapping is always first, from the first infinity to the last. Tapping is the crux of dance and dance is the crux of life. Learn to tap, your guru says, and everything else will follow.

That's why the first thing you learn in dance class is how to count under your breath. '*One*, two, three…beat…*one*, two, three….' You have to say it out loud; your hot breath mingles with sweat and stale deodorant. If you don't, numbers don't form fully and rhythm eludes you. '*One*, two, three….' Soon, the numbers slip from your mouth easily and you know the count the way you know the words of *The Very Hungry Caterpillar*, although you haven't yet learned how to read.

Finally, when your limbs remember the steps faster than you can, your guru pats your back for the first time. Although her figure has bloated with the years, she is a dancer herself. She pretends to wear her curves sensually and knows the value of this moment.

'Congratulations,' she tells you. 'You're on your way.'

But don't forget to bend your knees. Make sure your hands are behind your waist and that your palms bend outwards.

Tapping matters. But not as much as you thought it did.

Step Two: *Natta Adavu* (Stretching)

Stretch. Stretch until your calves quiver, until the balls of your feet sweat, until they melt into to the rubbery floor. Lean as the Earth leans.

By now, you are a dance veteran. At four, you joined the class with your horde of friends-since-birth, all smooth feet and curls. Indian parents have a need to push their children: karate for Karans and kathak for Kirans. But, as feet grew blisters and hair grew frizzy, your friends started to vanish, one by one. Now, it's just you and five other girls in the dingy gym rented from the local basketball team for one hour, Wednesday nights only. Five other girls who don't mind standing on their tippy toes until their nails crumble and peel. Who don't mind tightening their buns until their heads ache and throb. Who, like you, know that this doesn't matter. Because when you can tell stories with your eyes and hands, how could anything else matter?

Step Three: *Visharu Adavu* (Swinging)

This is the step where you begin to wish you really were a goddess and not just playing one, so you would have arms enough to accommodate the moves. It's the hardest part, according to your guru. If you can do this, you can do anything. Balance your arms in the lotus position; they may burn and shiver, but that just shows you're doing it right. Slowly, you realize your hands are no longer part of you. They have a will of their own.

'Good,' your guru says, and her smile is not forced. Her eyes are still the eyes of a dancer—dark and expressive, like yours should be. Open wide for a smile. Lashes fluttering for femininity. Slanted cheekily for character.

After a year, you can wrap a sari like an expert and shame on you if you haven't already mastered the art of kajal. Stories are important, your guru says. But you need to look the part as well. After all, Princess Sita would never have been seen with smeared lipstick.

Oh, and don't forget to smile.

Step Four: *Tattimetti Adavu* (Balancing)

Next, balance. You stand in the same position for so long that you begin to feel twinges in places you didn't know twinges could happen. Your backside cramps every day, but your mother ices your spine and you harden your mind.

This is the year that your dance class moves out of the gym and into a small red-brick building all to itself, with an official sign and business cards to its name. Suddenly, your guru is more serious about everything. No stray smudges of mascara, no tiny tremors of positions. This is her business now, and you are her client. You wonder what happened to the woman your mother used to invite over for tea.

You dance in a studio now. The walls are hospital white and the girls are just shadows on their surfaces. Mirrors are everywhere—there are two, three, too many to count—they must stretch into infinity. There's a moment, in the middle of a twirl, when your smile is shattered, scattered, across the panes of glass. You learn, all of five years old and already told you are cumbersome, to dance against the shadows, between the cracks where mildew grows. There, where one mirror ends and the other has not yet begun, you learn to lose yourself in a pivot.

Step Five: *Teermanam Adavu* (Ending)

Your guru's hair is newly cut and highlighted with streaks of light brown, so she has to blow it heavily out of her eyes when she criticizes you now. Illogically, this softens the blow of the insult. 'Big smiles,' she reminds you. 'This is the happy ending.'

The endings are always happy.

As you pose for the ending, arms raised high in the air, you feel the weight of an invisible book in your hands. If you were to open it, it would shine in the dim light of the stage. It's hard to read the words inside, but easy to imagine them.

Your mother couldn't come to watch this show; she is the on-call nurse at the hospital, and your father is away on business in Singapore. Before she dropped you off, she kissed your cheek and told you that you looked like a princess in your costume. You disagree—in a too-big sari that's tapered in all the wrong places, you look like an upside-down ice cream cone—but you smiled back at her anyway. So now you wait in the parking lot, watching as proud parents hug accomplished daughters and drive off into the hazy afternoon sun.

Molting grey pigeons perch on the sidewalk beside your battered flip-flops, scratching words you don't understand into the dirt. Together, you wait for a new day.

Step Six: *Sarikal Adavu* (Sliding)

It doesn't seem logical that you learn to slide after you learn to finish. Your guru tells you that this is because there is a grace to the slide that can only come from experience.

This is a lie, you learn quickly. The slide isn't an art—it's a calculation. It translates movements into variables, renders your actions generic, contoured to any form. Your body is linear, the y-axis of a Cartesian plane, and the three points of your head, chest and torso are distributed evenly and vertically. Symmetry matters. Poetry doesn't. Your body, boiled down to degrees of measured space.

Before, school was a temporary station in between dance classes. But the quiet boy two rows down from you in biology class has changed that. He is like no one you've ever seen before, with steely eyes and a face of planes and angles. You admire him the way women admire men who know they are to be admired.

'Everything is dying!' your teacher proclaims excitedly, jolting you out of your daydreams as she tries in vain to hammer the concept of entropy into the brains of summer-ready students.

She's overstating the concept. You know, because you've read ahead in the textbook. Everything isn't dying; it's simply changing. One state to another. Ice melts, then boils. It is far easier to be many things than it is to be one.

Step Seven: *Kudittametta Adavu* (Leaping)

The final step is the leap. This is a dancer's pride and joy. This is the step that differentiates mediocre from good, good from excellent. The day you master the leap, your head spins in giddiness. This is it. You are a dancer. It's done. You know you've nailed it, because after a performance, a bird-like woman with bright lip-gloss hands you a business card. 'Your dance is art,' she tells you. 'We need young dancers like you.'

Your guru offers you a tight-lipped smile. 'Congratulations,' she says, and for the first time since you can remember, her eyes are empty.

After the woman walks away, you pointedly throw the card in the trash, making sure that your guru can see. She pretends that she can't.

The boy's name is Alex, and he likes football. You realize the minute he asks you out that it's a mistake, but you say yes anyway. Sweaty palms. Nervous giggles. You kiss like a rooster; you lost your feathers in the fight. Your eyes muted, as you paint yourself with papier-mâché.

After you end things with him, you quit dance. Your guru's eyes betray no emotion, but you can see glimpses of who you used to be reflected in their hollow spaces.

On your way out, you think you see the shadow of a woman, a dancer, silhouetted against the wall. Light hits it, and she dissipates. Particles in the air. Dust you swallow when you're struggling to breathe. A heartbeat thuds in the background, but it is not your own. You forget that you must tap to it.

One, two, three...beat...*one*, two, three...

Ash

For the first time, Aishwarya is delighted when the TSA officer stops her in the airport security line.

'Please step aside, ma'am.'

'No problem, sir.'

On the monitor behind him, Ash's silhouette fills the screen; her stomach is yellow, her arms, green. Ash wonders, vaguely, what she could possibly be hiding there. The only bomb she'd ingested recently was the burrito bowl that wasn't quite sitting well in her stomach.

'Is this your bag, ma'am?'

'Yes, sir.'

When he rips open her backpack, running gloved fingers down her panties and rattling her makeup bag so that glass perfume bottles clink together precariously, she can only grin.

'Something funny, ma'am?'

'No, sir.'

She waits as he swabs her computer, opens and sniffs her acne medication. Finally, he finds it: the small jar of Bonne Maman Jam filled with some decidedly un-jamlike black dust. He shakes it; his many chins shake with him.

'What is this, ma'am?'

Ash finally lets herself laugh.

'My grandma, sir.'

Kathakali

Hands slippery. Mouths pizza-greasy.

When he first flirts with elastic, you say, 'No, not yet.' There's that sick stench coating your throat. But fingers demand what words do not. Persistent. Insistent.

'Don't worry, you'll like it.'

Resistant.

Inside you, the Kathakali man begins spinning.

Back home, the Kathakali dance mask hangs in your stairwell. The guardian to the kitchen when you're going downstairs; the gatekeeper to your bedroom going upstairs.

A tribute from your immigrant parents to the land they still call home.

The Kathakali man dances out the stories of your people. Tales of love and loss and war and death, told through taut hands, tapping feet. His green face-paint and red, shifting eyes express the pain of centuries. A symbol of your heritage, a constant of your culture, his ancient spinning filled your childhood nightmares. Years later, you met him again. Smiling, as always, on a jar of mango jam, in Target's 'International aisle'. Trapped in glass, he was still, for once—limbs frozen in incomplete twirls. Patel Brothers' Mango Jam, he proclaimed. *Bursting with the authentic regional flavours of India!* The f reverberates: *fff-flavour.*

Kyle from Tinder unhooks your bra. You hadn't even realized he'd touched you there.

When you first met him, you made small talk over lattes. The classes you're in, the places you'll go. You learn that he's studying to be an engineer. He wants to work for NASA. He seemed sweet, a little awkward. Harmless. A pimple—red-green, Christmas colours—was about to erupt on his cheek. He covered it, self-consciously, as he spoke. Somehow, this endeared him to you. Three dates later, when you suggested going home with him, his eyes and mouth opened wide. Like you were something precious. Like he'd won the lottery.

Now, suddenly, he smiles down at you. He looks like a Velociraptor. All teeth and bones. He looks like he could hurt you. Your body, hot and cold. Rough with goosebumps. Bra unhooked, ears buzzing, head fuzzy. Throat raw with knotted words.

The Kathakali man's wide skirts billow into your lungs. Green face, red eyes. Open arms receive your silent screams.

When Kyle from Tinder moves on top of you, your heart clangs in the vast emptiness of your chest. Sweat slithers. Fingers fumble. Skin sloshes against skin.

You concentrate on the Kathakali man dancing with your intestines, transforming them into red ribbons on his stage. To his audience, the ribbons become the swords of the fabled Chekavar warriors. Slicing out of your skin and into the sun. The battle-cries of your people.

'God.' Kyle pushes off you. Sweating. Smiling. Air fills your chest, suddenly and sharply. 'You're a good fuck.' *Fff-fuck.*

On Target's glass jar, the Kathakali Man grins and grins. Inside you, the Kathakali Man spins and spins. When he stops, the world is still.

Green face. Red eyes. The stories of your ancestors. The nightmares of your childhood. Infused, now, with Authentic Regional Flavour.

What do you taste when you look at me?

The Juvenile Immigrant

Arjun wakes me up one minute before my alarm goes off at seven, just like he has every day this week.

'Get up,' he says, flicking the light switch on and off three times. 'Time to run.'

My eyes start to water; I squeeze them shut. 'It's *Saturday*, Arjun! Do we have to run on a Saturday?'

'One-seventh of your life is a Saturday,' he says matter-of-factly. 'Do you want to waste one-seventh of your life?'

Without looking up, I know that he's slouching against the doorway, eyebrows slightly raised, fingers tapping rhythmically against his wrist. I also know he's not going to go away until he gets what he wants, so I squint into the harsh fluorescence and promise to be ready soon.

By the time I head downstairs, Arjun has already begun his breakfast. A pedometer is strapped smartly to his wrist, and a jogging jacket zipped right up to his neck, revealing fat bulging out at odd angles.

'Finally,' he says, not meeting my gaze when he talks, too focused on his bowl of Cheerios. 'You took forever.'

'I took five minutes,' I retort. But it's no use arguing with him. It's never any use arguing with him.

Arjun is silent as I grab my own bowl from the top shelf, but I see him wince when he hears the rattle of cereal falling. The pregnant pause, followed by the sloshing of milk, only twists his grimace further.

'Stop!' he cries out finally, standing up so that his chair wobbles underneath him. 'Just stop it!'

I mutter the sort of hasty sorry that most people would have seen right through. I know it's not his fault. It's not his fault that the noise bothers him so much, that everything bothers him so much. I know it, but I don't have to like it.

We eat our identical bowls of cereal in silence. I try to chew as quietly as possible, shifting the soggy rings to the back of my mouth and keeping my lips firmly closed. Arjun is slurping his milk by the spoonful. When he's done, he leaves the bowl on the table for me to clean up, and draws three precise lines through *7:00 a.m.: Eat breakfast* on the magnetic whiteboard that clings to the fridge. He smudges off the stray Expo marker debris, and looks at me expectantly.

Arjun's last pediatric check-up went like this: The mustachioed Dr Singh, whom Arjun always eyed warily because of his 'monkey beard', came in, smiled too broadly, and proclaimed, 'Wow, what a handsome young man you're turning into! You must be eating your veggies!' He grinned even wider when Arjun only scowled and mumbled under his breath in response.

Turning to my mother, Dr Singh gave Arjun's file a brief glance and decided, a little too quickly, 'Everything looks great, Mrs Chopra! We'll need him in for the usual tests in about a month, but for now, he's good to go!'

My mother's fingers relaxed on mine, fresh pink flooding out the metallic gray hues in her nails. 'Thank you, Dr Singh,' she said, and each syllable sagged under her relief. 'We were just worried, because he's been having a little trouble at school, gaining a little weight, and—'

'What?' Arjun's head snapped towards my mother, his bushy eyebrows pushing against each other in an unusual display of focus. 'I have been?'

The doctor waved her concern away, somehow maintaining his plastered-on smirk as he simpered, 'No, no, nothing to worry about, Mrs Chopra. A few pounds here and there is normal for a teenager his age. It's the hormones, you know. You'll see, it'll all melt off in the blink of an eye!'

But once Arjun has something in his head, there's nothing and no one that can talk him out of his plans. When he came home that day, he frantically paced around the house, counting his steps, counting the jiggles of his stomach, counting his beats per minute.

'You're right,' he finally told my mother, after three hours of pacing. 'I'm overweight. I need to lose weight. Help me lose weight.'

And this was my mother's plan of attack: You need to exercise, because you'll never lose weight sitting on the couch all day. But you can't run by yourself, not in this neighbourhood—it wouldn't be safe. Kiran will run with you! After all, it's not like she can't afford to lose a few pounds herself. If you do it every morning, Kiran, you'll get used to it. You'll even start to enjoy it!

So, here I am, trailing after Arjun, my sneakers hitting the ground in weary thumps. Expecting, at every turn, a man wielding a gun, brandishing it at our heads. *You can't run here, brown girl!*

One...two...three...*no.* I resist the urge to count the steps out loud. I resist the urge so hard that the numbers well up inside me, and I turn them into multiplication tables instead. Anything but counting. Anything but counting in threes.

Two times two is four.

Three times three is nine.

Arjun is running ahead of me, like he always does. I can't escape his stoic huffs, even from back here. I concentrate on the running, on the numbers. I synchronize the rhythmic slaps of my shoes to my heartbeat. I try to pretend that my feet aren't saying 'cray-zy, cray-zy' with every crash against the concrete. It makes me fast, and skilled at math. And very much alone.

Three years ago, we bought the house dirt-cheap, because the Muslim family who lived here before us was desperate to leave. Right after my father signed on the dotted line, Akbar, the previous owner, looked at us pityingly.

'Listen, there's something you should know about this neighbourhood,' he told us, reaching into the inner pocket of his coat. He pulled out a stack of loose-leaf papers, filled with angry black-ink scrawl and bound together with rubber bands. They were flimsy and ragged, like they'd been pulled out of a child's notebook.

'We've been getting these in our mailbox for the past two years,' he said. Craning my neck, I could just make out the words *get the fuck out of my country* and *fuck your allah.* I was twelve at the time, and had to stifle the giggles that bubbled up my throat from reading *fuck* so many times. I remember asking my father the next day who Allah was, and why anyone would want to fuck him. I remember being told to watch my mouth in response.

'We don't know who's sending them. We don't know if they're dangerous—I hope they're not—but I thought you should know,' Akbar said. 'I just didn't feel like it's a safe place to bring up my kids. They're so little now, but one day, this will start to affect them too.'

My father's reply was vague, or maybe it's just my memory. After struggling for years to get a green card and finally securing a well-paying IT job that wouldn't leave his family hungry, he wasn't about to let a few poorly-written letters scare him off. He said something along the lines of: 'Thank you for telling us. I'm sorry you had to deal with that, but I'm not expecting it to be a problem—we're not Muslim.'

I've been told I look like my mother: dark-skinned, tight-lipped, small-breasted, hair too wild for straighteners. I've been told we're alike so often, I've started to forget that it's not true. Watching her bustle around the kitchen, work-wrinkled fingers fluttering like small birds, I remember that my mother and I are different. I remember that she gave up a six-figure salary to take care of her child when he needed her, that all she has to show for her background in software development is her 180 words-per-minute typing speed. I remember that she's necessary.

'Amma, I'm sorry,' I say, obligingly licking chutney off the spoon she stretches out to me. 'It needs more salt. Anyway, I couldn't run with him today. I had an exam to study for.'

'You could have studied after,' my mother says, expertly pinching a mound of dough into a perfect dome. 'Besides, wasn't this a calculus exam? Why weren't you already prepared?'

I roll my eyes and pick at the burnt edges of the discarded roti pile, filled with black Rorschach-test air bubbles. The ones too imperfect to serve to my father. The rejects are probably the reason Arjun and I have to run so much.

But she's right; I didn't really need to study for the exam. Numbers come easily to me. They unwrap in my mind like shiny italicized gifts—easily recognized, easily understood. I take comfort in the company of their patterns, their rhythms, their predictability. It's something that Arjun and I have in common. It's something I wish we didn't.

'Yes, that's what I thought,' my mother says knowingly, taking my silence as an answer and shoving another spoon of chutney in my mouth. It's minty and grainy, and not meant to be eaten by itself. 'You're just lazy and didn't want to run. Don't try to fool me, Kiran. I gave birth to you. I know math is too easy for you. You're just like Arjun. You two and your numbers!'

The chutney burns my mouth, and I swallow it forcefully, along with the words I want to scream at her: *No, I'm not like Arjun, because he's crazy and I'm not.* 'The chutney's perfect, Amma,' I say instead. 'No more salt—or mirchi, please.'

She smiles a little, crinkling the hollows under her eyes. 'You know it's never spicy enough for the boys.' But still, she tucks the chilli powder back in the cabinet. The tight sleeves of her blouse create a permanent red bangle on her upper arms, leaving loose skin to swing around her armpits like wings when she reaches up to grab a mixing spoon.

'Speaking of the boys, where's Arjun?' I ask, my focus back on the roti. 'Isn't his bus supposed to be here by now?'

My mother swivels, her eyebrows scrunched into a close-knit V-formation. 'You're right. He was supposed to be here half an hour ago. He hasn't called, or texted.' She scrutinizes her phone, bringing it so close that her breath fogs its screen, as though squinting at it will reveal hidden messages from her son.

'I can go check the stop, if you want,' I offer. It's an empty one. I know she'll want to go herself. The roti dough lies forgotten on the counter, as she tugs off her apron without washing her flour-whitened hands.

'No—but come with me, please,' she asks, and I'm about to roll my eyes, to say snarky hilarities like *why, you think you might die if you walk down the street alone?* But I stop myself, the words fizzing against my tongue. I stop myself when I see the glint of genuine fear in her eyes. Maybe she does think that. Maybe we all do.

Outside, the Texas sun is suffocating. At once damp and dry, the heat seeps everywhere, in everything, leaving behind a blistering trail of parched mouths, sweaty shirts, fuzzy heads. Arjun's stop is all the way at the end of the block, five minutes from our house. But that doesn't stop my mother from screaming for him the second we close the door.

'Arjun! Arjun beta?'

We hear him before we see him.

'Here, here.' His voice is bored, almost. Tired.

He's huddled on the curb, using his sweater and backpack as a makeshift seat. 'Where have you been?' he asks accusingly.

'What do you mean, where have we been? Where have you

been? Why didn't you come home?'

'The bus didn't come.' Flat tone. Flat affect.

'What?' My mother stops in her tracks, and I stumble to a halt beside her.

'The bus didn't come.'

Arjun's bus arrives at 8:00 on the dot, and he's always there to greet it. But this morning, after the run I skipped out on, he knocked over the bowl of cereal he'd left half-eaten earlier. Mushy Cheerios disintegrated into the carpet, leaving wood-chip crumbs everywhere he stepped.

This did not comply with his routine. This did not compute. With my mother in the shower, he could only stand there helplessly, before it occurred to him to call me for help. 'Kiran! I need you! There's a spill!'

And I refused to come downstairs. 'Check your cleaning list! Call me if you still need help after.'

Arjun's cleaning list, penned in my mother's neat, full handwriting, reads like this:

1. Breathe deeply, in and out.
2. Check the third cabinet from the fridge. Find cleaning supplies.
3. Wipe the mess up. If something spilled on the floor or on the counter, spray with Clorox and wipe.

But it wasn't this simple. There were other commands involved, commands my mother had forgotten to outline.

4. Shove everything back into the cabinet and close the door quickly, before the cleaning supplies and condiment bottles come crashing down on you.
5. Hurry, hurry, because the noise will hurt your ears.
6. Move quickly, or else they will fall around you, clanging loudly, destroying the perfect symmetry of the square floor tiles.
7. Sit there, among the rubble, holding your hands over your ears, rocking back and forth three times a second, trying to impose something resembling order on the situation.

This was how I found him: knees pulled up to his chest, hands clasped tightly over his ears, tears clinging precariously to his eyelashes. Seeing him there—sixteen years old and still a baby, still more like the nuisance of a toddler that I babysit than my older brother, the person who's supposed to protect me, support me, care for me—I couldn't identify the emotion that knotted my stomach. Was it pity? Disdain? I couldn't tell, and didn't waste too much time trying to puzzle it out. Instead, I silently wiped the floor, handed Arjun a granola bar, and waved him out the door.

This morning, he left the house at 8:10. This morning, he missed the bus. This morning, he waited eight hours at the bus stop for a bus that was never going to come, a bus that had left him behind a long time ago.

My mother doesn't say a word. She rubs Arjun's shoulder, pulls him up by the hand. 'Time to come home, beta,' she murmurs, patting his hands, 'Let me get some food in you.'

He agrees mutely, letting her pull him up by the wrist. I lag behind the two of them on the way home, slightly embarrassed to be seen with the teenager holding his mother's hand, slightly guilty about my embarrassment. Until something strikes me. 'Arjun, why were you waiting on this side of the road? The bus stop is in front of Mr Harvey's house, isn't it?'

Arjun turns around, his features still slack and unresponsive. 'Yes, but I had to move. Mr Harvey told me not to sit in front of his house anymore.'

'What do you mean? That's where the bus picks you up.'

'Yes, but he says I can't sit there anymore, because it's his property. It makes sense, Kiran. It's his property. He owns it. Like how you can't play with my cars, and I can't touch your makeup.'

I frown. From this distance, Mr Harvey's silhouette is just about visible through his partly drawn blinds. He's eating alone, like always, and on a normal day, my mother would cluck her tongue in pity.

'What a nice man,' she'd say. 'So sad he never found a wife.'

Today, though, we exchange glances, but say nothing.

I once spoke to my mother about who the letter-writer could be, back when we first moved in. We'd never gotten a letter ourselves, but I always had a morbid fascination with them. We sat down, wrote up a list, crossed off several names—Mr Hernandez was part-Latino, the Johnson family moved away, the McKennas were registered Democrats. With only two people left to go, my mother put her hand on my wrist, stopping my pen from going any further. Between the two of them—one a lawyer with amiable eyebrows fading into his receding hairline, the other, Mr Harvey, a lonely grandpa who nurtured his rose garden with such tenderness—I think she decided it was better that we didn't find out.

'Besides,' she told me, in a too-bright tone, 'We're not Muslim. We're not even religious. Don't worry so much about little things, Kiran. Good things happen to good people.'

This year, Arjun's birthday falls on a Monday, a school-day. We're celebrating on a Sunday, a day we're all at home, a day we can devote to him. Too bad the birthday boy can't understand this logic.

'But it's not my birthday,' he insists, even as we bake him a cake, even as we show him the pile of presents we've gotten him. 'My birthday is tomorrow. My birthday is Monday.'

Still, he grins when he opens my gift—another installment of our running comic strip, *Arjun the Invisible Man*, featuring a rip-off Harry Potter invisibility cloak, my brother as a crime-fighting superhero, and me as his right-hand man, Kick-ass

Kiran. Naturally, the supervillain for this issue had to be our mother. Yesterday, Arjun had a fight with her over her insistence on washing his favourite sweatshirt.

'It's lucky,' he'd tried to tell her. 'You'll wash away the luck.' He tugged it away from her and over his head, and has since refused to take it off.

In the comic, my mother, Chanda the Terrible, terrorizes Arjun's school as a demonic principal who makes kids come to class on weekends and assigns mountains of homework. Arjun the Invisible Man sneaks into the school after dark, slipping past security easily, and writes every student an absence letter excusing them for the rest of the year. The whole school celebrates their mysterious hero.

'It's good,' he pronounces when he's finished reading—some of the highest praise I've ever heard him utter. 'I wish I could really do this. But invisibility cloaks don't exist in real life, only in stories.'

His smile is lopsided, one side higher than the other as he touches the page to his nose to contemplate the cover sketch. My chest feels tight. I pull him into a hug before he can protest, burying my nose into a sweatshirt in desperate need of a wash. Arjun hates being hugged, so I'm surprised when I feel three quick pats on my forearm that, from anyone else, would feel clinical.

'Thank you, Kick-ass,' he says, and we both burst into giggles, because 'ass' is a bad word, one of the words Arjun has promised to never, ever say.

Later that night, we're driving to the bakery. We made the wrong type of marble cake. Arjun likes chocolate with vanilla swirled in; we made vanilla with chocolate swirled in. We miss our exit, which Arjun points out two seconds before our GPS does.

'Damn,' my father says.

'Damn, damn, damn,' Arjun repeats, and we giggle again.

We make the U-turn just as we hear little clacks on the roof of the car. Hazy raindrops stick against the windows, rolling off their own reflections into glassy blackness. I draw Arjun's superhero character in the rain-fogged glass, breaking it down into geometry, into easily-replicable circles and lines. He's fascinated, watching my finger turn art into math and back again.

'Will you teach me?' he asks.

Yes, I say. Yes, I will.

When it gets dark, we watch the superhero illuminate, glowing under the red lights of the highway.

On Monday, Arjun wakes me up one minute before my alarm goes off at seven, just like he has every day for the past two months.

'Get up,' he says, flicking the light switch on and off three times. 'Time to run.'

'Arjun, it's your birthday!' I exclaim in a futile attempt to distract him, my face still hidden under the covers. 'Happy birthday!'

'We celebrated yesterday, so we can't say that today. It wouldn't be fair. No one gets two birthdays,' Arjun says. His jacket zipped. His pedometer flashing. Ready.

'Arjun, please. Not today. Tomorrow, definitely. Not today. It's a Monday, and it's your birthday. You shouldn't even run—take a day off!'

Arjun frowns, taps his fingers against his stomach. 'I can't. I ate so much cake. Too much cake, more cake than I was allowed to eat.'

I sit up in bed, stretching my arms until they click. 'Listen, if you let me sleep, I swear I'll teach you how to draw your superhero character tonight. Promise.'

'Pinky promise?'

'Pinky promise.'

As soon as Arjun turns off the light, I close my eyes again in anticipation of the precious half-hour of sleep I'll get before my non-human alarm clock wakes me up.

Instead, twenty minutes later, I jolt awake to my mother's scream.

This is what the news articles said, after it happened:

Matthew Harvey, 72, woke up to a threatening knock on the door at an odd hour in the morning. He was confronted by a tall, burly foreign man who said something in a language that he couldn't understand. The man made intimidating gestures, and acted as though he were trying to get into the house. Matthew Harvey had no choice. He had to shoot him. He was standing his ground. Considering all legal precedents, the news anchors assure us, justice will be served and Matthew Harvey will be found innocent of all charges.

This is what the news articles missed:

My mother, curled into a fetal position on the floor, her harrowing, racking screams haunting our nights. My father, who found a pedometer lying in Harvey's yard two days after the shooting, who sits at the kitchen table every night when he thinks I'm asleep, staring at cupped hands that hold nothing but air. Me, smashing leftover birthday cake onto the floor, stuffing the cake in my mouth from the floor, chocolate and vanilla and dust and tears all mingling together. And then Harvey, currently in a minimum-security cell at the Travis County Jail, who, when asked why he didn't recognize that the boy knocking on his door was his neighbour, replied, 'How could I? They all look the same.'

We know the story is bullshit. We know that there's no way Arjun would knock on Harvey's door, not when he'd already been warned, not when it would mess up his routine. But there's no evidence that he was just in Harvey's yard, picking up his fallen pedometer. No security footage, no witnesses. No one to help us. No one to believe us.

The doctors say there's still a chance. Arjun is minimally responsive, but fMRI results show spikes of yellow against the pitch black of a broken brain. Spikes of yellow might mean reflex, or they might mean consciousness. It's too early to tell.

I go to the hospital right after school. I bring him flowers, even though he always thought they were stupid gifts. Pointless. They're going to die, anyway. I had an English pop quiz, and I tell him about it—about how hard it was, and who needs to know what the word zephyr meant in the context of *Moby Dick*, anyway? I read him the latest installments of our comic. His superpowers have grown, expanded into laser vision and telepathy. I curl my little finger around his, remembering the pinky promise that never was. His finger curls back, and although every part of my brain—my logical, mathematical, rational brain—knows it's just an instinctive response, I tell myself it's not.

A Love Story in 100 Words

When I was twelve, my father made a throwaway comment that haunted me for years: 'When I married your mother, I won.'

With light eyes, straight hair, and fair skin—the closest Indians get to whiteness—my mother is my opposite. I grew up painfully aware that, if my father was the winner of this game, *my* partner would be the loser.

But this year, for the first time, I fell for a woman. A woman who looks like me. On her, black eyes are inviting, coarse curls enticing. On her, darkness glows. In falling for her, I fell for myself. Hard.

Aaja Nachle

The first problem was the song choice. Payal wanted to dance to 'Desi Girl'; Noor voted for 'Aaja Nachle'.

The second problem was costume. Payal suggested a blue salwar; Noor preferred green.

The third problem, of course, was that Payal was Hindu and Noor was Muslim.

'Don't you see?' Payal's mother said. She was sitting on the sofa, Kurkure rustling in her lap, Zee TV on in the background. 'She wants green because she's Muslim. Don't let her win.'

Noor's mother, in turn, called blue tacky and predictable— just like Payal's family.

After school, every sixth-grade Talent Show entry was allowed to practice on the stage for half an hour. For twenty minutes, the girls bickered. For ten, they danced lukewarmly and asynchronously to their compromise song, 'Sheila ki Jawaani'. Later that afternoon, both of their mothers categorically forbade them from dancing to 'Sheila ki Jawaani', proving there were some things they could agree on, after all.

That night, Zee TV interrupted a rerun of *Ek Tha Raja, Ek Thi Rani* for a breaking news segment: an old man who looked like Payal's grandfather had been murdered in a lynching last night. Payal looked up from her assigned reading, an O'Henry story, to see that a mob had beaten both the man who looked like her grandfather and his son with stones and bricks. When the police came an hour later, the man was dead. His crime: eating beef.

'Chhi!' Payal's mother exclaimed, changing the channel to Star TV. 'He shouldn't have broken the law.'

The beef ban, Payal learned, had recently spread across North India, from the man's home in Uttar Pradesh to Payal's family home in Mumbai. It was a sign of something, Payal's father once tutted, but he never said of what.

Something churned inside Payal, not for the first time. She nodded mutely, fiddling with the buttons on her pajama sleeve. She had eaten a cheeseburger at McDonald's just two weeks ago. Her friend had ordered all the food for the group, and she hadn't wanted to make a fuss. She found the burger delicious, but forced herself to throw it up within minutes. It hadn't polluted her for too long. She was still good. Her parents would never know. When she crouched, retching, on the grimy McDonald's bathroom, staring at a rim of crusty brown staining the toilet bowl, Noor knelt beside her. Rubbing her back in circles and joking that she would tell on Payal to auntyji.

Noor had always been a better dancer than Payal. Enrolled in classical Indian dance lessons when she was seven years old, just a year before the girls met, she had now been dancing for five years. Participating for the Talent Show was her idea. Year after year, they watched their white classmates shimmy gracelessly to Katy Perry, and, finally, Noor had tired of it.

'Honestly, even if you suck, we'll probably win,' had been her way of convincing Payal to perform with her. 'Texans eat up Bollywood. It's like—exotic, or something.'

When they started, Noor already had choreography prepared for 'Aaja Nachle'. She'd found a video tutorial on YouTube, complete with bindi-speckled white girls, and executed the movements they made up better than they did. She moved fluidly, as though it were her limbs and not her brain that knew the music.

Payal raised a fuss, in part, out of jealousy. The movements didn't translate from her brain downwards. Her body was unruly in a way that Noor's was not. She was clumsier, heavier, more uncomfortably aware of how she took up space. The choreography for 'Desi Girl' was much more suited to her: twirling, hip-shaking. Lots of style, little substance.

It was clear something was wrong when Noor called instead of texted. They hadn't spoken on the phone since fourth grade, when Payal used to bury herself deep in her parents' walk-in closet, draped in dusty sweaters and musty dupattas, talking to Noor until her father's snores seeped through the crack in the door.

'Listen, um—' Noor's voice was wrong too. Different, somehow. 'I'm so sorry about this, but my mom says I can't do the talent show with you.'

Payal tried to sound shocked. 'Oh! What happened?'

There was a pause that lasted a little too long. Payal traced the pattern of crackling on the line: three pops, then a breath. 'Dude, I don't even know. I just can't. I'm sorry.'

She knew. Payal knew. And both knew the other knew.

'It's fine. Don't worry about it,' Payal said, after letting Noor stew in static for a few seconds. 'See you tomorrow?'

Noor's exhale was palpable, sliding through the cell phone like slime. 'Yup. See you tomorrow!'

At lunch, Payal ate with her friends from temple. Noor approached, mouth pursed as though she were about to say something. She turned without a word, sitting alone at their usual table, picking at her blue plastic tray. It was after biology, when Payal begged out of dissecting their shared rat, Ignacio, that Noor finally spoke up.

'Okay, what's going on?' she asked, leaning against Payal's locker. 'You've been acting weird all day.'

Payal opened the locker, staring slant-eyed at her reflection in the magnetic mirror on its door. 'I have not. You have.'

'Oh, I have?' Noor scoffed. She was slouching, but stood up straight now, her foot-tapping getting dangerously rapid. 'You know what, it's probably better that we didn't sit together at lunch, because guess what I had?' She leaned in closer, her breath hot in Payal's face. '*Beef.*'

The days leading up to the talent show were cautious and vast. Payal avoided Noor and found, with a twinge of sadness, that it was all too easy to do so—she had her schedule memorized, after all. She got out of her biology lab practical by claiming to be a religious vegetarian. Her teacher, a woman named Mrs Shelley who was red, nervous and wore her acrylic nails like armour, didn't dare to contest her. Payal got a take-home test, instead. Mr Jackson, the theatre teacher and the talent show coordinator, asked Payal in class how her dance was coming along.

'Oh—I'm not doing that anymore?' Her voice rose at the end, but Payal hadn't intended for it to be a question.

'That's strange,' Mr Jackson said. 'Your name is still on our sheet.'

Payal glanced down; this statement was only partly true. 'Noor and PayPal,' the sheet read. Still, seeing their names together on paper stung a little. She wondered if Noor had just forgotten to remove their names, but following some sleuthing from behind the cafeteria tables after school, she realized Noor planned on dancing solo. This stung even more.

'Payal beta, you made the right decision,' her mother said. 'These things with Muslims—they never end well.' She was still in her scrubs; that day, a patient had thrown up on her good clothes. 'I knew I should have been a doctor,' she'd told Payal earlier. 'Nobody throws up on doctors. Besides, I'm smarter than all of them.' After a moment of contemplation, she conceded, 'Although, if I were a doctor, we may never have gotten our green card...

'But listen, all you have to do is look at the news to realize that..... Look at what they're doing to the world. Such terror. They believe in it, too, you know. Jihad is in the Quran.' She said this in Hindi, and the words sounded ugly in her mouth.

Payal did look at the news. She looked at the news regularly. BBC was the homepage on her new smartphone. She worried she may be looking at it wrong, though. Because all the news told her that thousands of Muslims had been murdered in Gujarat. That the new Prime Minister championed the same ideas as Gandhi's murderer. That the current government wanted India to be a land for just Hindus. Only Hindus. That, maybe, for the first time in their lives, her parents were wrong. But that couldn't be. Could it?

The churning was worse now. It swayed her. It made her dizzy. She threw up, and told her mother it was from the cafeteria food—'Tch! I've told you not to eat that rubbish. And still you won't take the food I work so hard to make for you'. She grinned and lied and lied. As she knelt in front of the toilet, her hair fell into the bowl—vomit-coated, toilet-watered strings. She missed Noor's cool, dry hands brushing her hair away, rubbing her back. She missed Noor.

That night, she stayed up until her alarm went off at six-thirty. She watched dance tutorials to 'Aaja Nachle' until her vision blurred; she practised until her legs shook. At school, she sought Noor out, and found, with that same twinge of sadness, that it was harder than she expected. Than it had been just two weeks ago. Noor, it seemed, had moved on.

'Hey!' she said, a little too eagerly, a little too loudly, when she finally found Noor. Her smile trembled. 'Hey, I just realized—just now, literally, just now—that our names are still on the talent show sign-up sheet.' She held her breath. That came across as chill and breezy, didn't it?

Noor's gaze was cool. She was in the middle of the hallway, walking to class with a pony-tailed girl that Payal had never seen before. 'So?'

'So—I learned "Aaja Nachle" for you.' The words tumbled out, tripping over each other. 'I mean, since we're still technically signed up anyway, I figured, well, why not?'

Noor's eyes widened. Payal's heart beat faster. There were two agonizing seconds before Noor burst out into laughter. 'Oh my god, you idiot,' she said. 'I learned "Desi Girl" for *you*!'

They wound up compromising, again, settling on a YouTube remix of the two that they downloaded illegally. They didn't win the talent show. They didn't even place. Clearly, Texans didn't love Bollywood as much as Noor thought. When they snuck a peek at the judges' scorecards after the event, though, they saw the comment: 'The dance was a little awkward, but kudos to them—they were perfectly in sync.'

Enough

It occurs to him that the rain is the perfect place to hide his secrets. The wetness, like a celebration. Water racing to meet a ground that has been barren for too long, people that have been thirsty for too long. New rain on dirt, dry dust-coils lost in humid air. The heat has nothing to push against, nothing to beat. The rain will keep his secrets.

There was once a child who sat here, where he sits now, many years ago. It is still hard to believe that he was once that child. That this is the same lifetime. Round face, brown eyes. A girl beside him—maybe seven, maybe younger. A tree too, a guava one, but not thick like you might imagine. A skinny, tall plant with branches too weak for climbing, green fruit that never ripened. Her voice lisped when she talked, so she whispered instead. There isn't much he remembers from those days, but he can still remember her whispering, every time it rained: 'Do you want to dance?'

And he didn't, he never did. So he sat under the canopy, legs crossed in his father's bamboo chair that had begun to slant and splinter, watching. He liked the smell that swirled on days like this, just after the monsoon started. Almost as if the air had changed overnight, become cleaner, fresher. He watched as she twirled and twirled alone around the guava tree, pigtails unraveling, bare feet glistening. She twirled with her eyes closed, head tilted back to catch the raindrops in her mouth. They taste like they smell, she told him. Fresh, clean. But he never wanted to try.

The house is old now, not new like it was then, when his father had it built—almost twenty years ago. The people here have aged with it. The village is filled with greying heads and croaking voices. The young people are gone; they have fled to everywhere that is not here, because they can hear the voice of the succubus that seeps through the cracks of these doors like smoke tendrils, the voice his parents and their parents are deaf to. *'I have sung your name for centuries.'*

He has left too, he will not be trapped. This cramped corner of northern India, stuck in time for hundreds of years, with static-crackled telephones and dial-up Internet, is not for him. He has returned only for three days, at his mother's request, and he has told no one in the States where he is going. He is always ashamed to tell colleagues where he comes from when they ask—he will mumble, say Delhi, the city closest to here. They won't press him, but it always leaves him uncomfortable. Like he's hiding himself. Him and his rainy-day ghosts. He must remind himself that this isn't him. That child was not him; this man is not him. He is the software engineer for Google. He is the success story. The one that got out. He is not this man sipping tea on the porch where he once watched a little girl dance, eyes closed, head back. This man contemplating a fate he once considered worse than death.

That girl sits across from him now. She has a starched purple veil drawn over her head, jasmine woven in the plait underneath it, oily blackness against the petals. If he had met her on the street, he wouldn't have recognized her. The little girl she used to be had an unlined face, a willing grin that this woman's painted-pink smile cannot find. Her name is Anamika—a name that means 'nameless'.

He purses his lips, smiles at her. Inside, their parents are chatting politely over a table filled with samosas. He knows what this is. His mother has, on several occasions, expressed her concern that he is in his thirties, still unmarried. Sighing, he attempts to strike up a conversation. 'I remember,' he begins, 'we played here together, when we were very young. You used to sneak away and come visit me, even though your parents scolded you later. Do you remember?'

She looks down demurely, away from the sheets of rain just beyond the porch. 'Yes.' Her Hindi is better than his. More formal, every syllable enunciated. For just a second, he feels a twinge of jealousy.

Looking over at the house next-door—the shabby one, with the rusting gate and untamed weeds growing from cracks in fences—he asks, keeping his voice as nonchalant as possible, 'And do you remember him? The boy next door, Dev, who used to come and play with us sometimes? Does his family still live there?'

She looks up, manicured eyebrows almost meeting in surprise. 'No,' she says, 'they moved away, long ago. Why do you ask?'

She doesn't say it, but he knows that he is treading the lines of propriety. Their neighbours were poor, much poorer than them. Years ago, the boy's mother had worked for his mother.

He nods, closes his eyes. He tries to lean his head back against the bamboo chair like he used to when he was a child, but finds that he is now much too tall.

Silence, now. Stillness. The rain-smell is heavy, and he thinks to himself that he would run, if the weather were better. He's very strict about exercise at home; he has three pairs of white Nikes in a row next to his door. When he gets bored of one pair, he wears another. Back in San Francisco, he and a friend go running every morning, or close to that, amid smoke, crowds, staring homeless people and pointing teenagers laughing at the two pot-bellied men chasing after their youth. Of course, that sight would be out of place here. Who would care to see his tight T-shirts, his expensive track pants—surely the trees and the villagers have no interest in his wealth. His discipline. So he decides to hold off on running, at least until he returns.

They make small talk, he and this woman who used to be a girl. Talk about the aunty a few houses down, who died recently of cancer, and the audacity of her children, who moved her widowed husband to a home instead of having him stay with them. About the priest of their childhoods, recently accused of child molestation but never convicted. About her, Anamika, who started a BA in college but never finished.

After a while, the rain slows to a drizzle, then stops altogether. The sky is a darker shade of grey, and mosquitoes begin buzzing in the after-rain humidity. They go inside, where her parents are standing in the entrance hall, shuffling around their slippers, ready to leave. He says it was a pleasure to see them again, and they enthusiastically reciprocate. They should meet again, he says. They look slyly at their daughter and agree.

After they are gone, his mother begins picking up their dishes. They ate all the samosas, she remarks. Don't they know that's rude? His father sits back down on the divan, switches the TV to a cricket test match.

'How did you like the girl?' his father asks, without taking his eyes off the screen.

'She's fine,' he replies, truthfully. She was fine. He goes to his room and stretches out on his thinning mattress. He can feel the wooden panes of the bedframe pressing into his back. He wonders if he should call Varun—his roommate, his running buddy—and tell him that maybe, for him, fine could be enough. But he figures there's no point upsetting him just yet.

He decides the next morning to postpone his departure. Pulling out his mobile phone—it's a new model, one he's proud to let his parents *ooh* and *aah* over—he calls his office, tells them he'll be extending his leave for the next two weeks. His voice is firmer out loud than in his head. He speaks like a man who has made up his mind. His mother is ecstatic; his father, silent.

Anamika becomes more open the more time he spends with her. She tells him excitedly about her plans for her wedding; she still refers to it as hers, not theirs. Indian girls cannot afford to be forward. She wants arches of marigold blossoms in the doorways, a three-course meal for the guests with both vegetarian and non-vegetarian options. A red silk sari for the ceremony, a turquoise one for the reception. Fragrant biryani beaded with black spices, mehndi patterns that twist up to her elbows. When she speaks like this, he sees the tiniest light in her eyes, an almost forgotten spark. If he squints a little, he can imagine her with a lisp, asking him if he wants to dance.

One afternoon, when his parents are asleep and the house is quiet, he pulls on his tennis shoes and walks around the area. When he was younger, he would pretend he was an adventurer, one of the men he read about in his American books and magazines. Exploring a new land, conquering it. Alone and triumphant. He would pretend to discover new species of the same beetles and snakes, exclaim over 'exotic' bird-calls that he had heard thousands of times before. It made him feel like he wasn't from this place, but was instead uncovering it—the wild beauty of rural India. Like he didn't really belong here at all.

Rocks crunch underneath his feet as he tries hard to remember. There is his old fourth-standard teacher's house, the woman who once smacked a girl with a ruler for wearing her hair in one plait instead of two. There is the old church, from which prayers used to emanate every morning and every evening. There, the fish-market. There, the bazaar. Somehow, all too quickly, he ends up where he started. Not at his house, but at Dev's, the shack next-door. He decides to go knock on the door, for the sake of nostalgia, if nothing else.

While he is waiting for a response, he looks around. Like everything else, this hasn't changed much. Same peeling white-grey paint on the bricks. Same bare windows, covered by nothing more than a mosquito-net. He even thinks he spies the same black stray cat skulking around the back, the one he and Dev made fat with all their leftovers.

A woman opens the door, stringy hair falling out of a haphazard bun. She seems shocked, even a little nervous, to see him, wiping her hands on her already stained nightie. She's been cooking, she explains. He smiles at her, introducing himself as Pandey saab's son. Her eyes grow wide and he realizes that, in all the years that they had been neighbours, his parents have never bothered to visit her. Upon her invitation, he walks inside and sits on the plastic-covered armchair she points him to.

'I'll make you some tea,' she insists, after laying a platter of Parle-G biscuits on the coffee table in front of him. 'It's not every day I have visitors. I'll make you some tea.'

He's happy to agree, to hear, to remember. Dev's family, he learns, moved to Delhi, almost four years ago. She and her husband have been living here since. Her husband is an overseer, she adds proudly. They have three children, all grown and, unfortunately, all girls.

She clatters around in the tiny kitchen, fixing him far more than the promised cup of tea, and he studies the house he once knew so well. Almost every day after school, he had come over here to play with Dev, his friend mostly because his parents couldn't stand what he was. They couldn't understand his determination to befriend their servant's son, which, of course, made him all the more stubborn in pursuing the friendship.

In all honesty, however, he and Dev had little in common. Dev went to an inferior government school, where English was not emphasized and teachers were lethargic. He had no ambitions or desires, it seemed, except movies. He loved movies. He loved all of them: comedies, dramas, tragedies, romances. Going to Mumbai, to Bollywood, was his most treasured dream. He had no grand illusions of becoming a hero; no, as he often said, 'a role as an extra would do just fine.'

He used to think that Dev could do it. He was handsome, as a boy, with fair skin and dark curly hair.

Once, during one of his many after-school visits, he and Dev were sitting on the stairwell, poring over a magazine. 'Man, look at her lips,' Dev was saying, gazing longingly at a glossy cover-spread of Rekha. 'Don't you just want to kiss them?'

He nodded, more out of convenience than interest. It was starting to concern him, his apathy to these sorts of things. He'd always considered Dev's obsession just that, an obsession. But maybe it was he who was odd, not Dev.

That's when it happened. At the same time Dev leaned in to turn the page, he turned his head to look down at the picture. His lips grazed the skin of Dev's cheeks, near his nose, near his mouth, and suddenly, the cramped staircase felt suffocating. But it was nothing. An accidentally, barely-there, hardly-anything nothing. Dev laughed, made a face, said, 'I meant Rekha, not you.' He tried to laugh too, but his chest felt too tight to let him. He dug his nails into his sweaty palms, looked away, and willed his ears to stop pulsing.

That night, he lay awake, listening to the rain and the crickets outside. It was hot, humid, almost, but he still pulled the sheet up to his chin, gripped it tightly with trembling fingers. Somewhere in his neighbourhood, someone had lit their garbage on fire, and dying curls of smoke seeped under

his open window, muddling the mustiness of rain. *Rain-spell,*
smoke-smell, keep my secrets. Keep my shame.

He remembers this now, as he stares at the darkened
corridors, the green geckos plastered to the walls. This house
is a witness to truths that need no reminding, memories that
grow and contract upon contact. He needs no witnesses.

Thanking the woman, he drinks his tea fast, in big gulps
with hands that have grown older but still tremble the same
way. He knows now that he should not have come.

He goes back to the States and returns seven months later. He
and Anamika are now formally engaged. Varun has moved
out of their flat.

Before he came back to this village, before even his mother
had telephoned him, asking him to come back, he had
realized that there were two possibilities for his future. Two,
and they lay sprawled in front of him—two different paths,
two different destinations—each equally unappealing, each
decidedly unsatisfying. He had to choose one.

There could be a wife. In these empty rooms of his house,
in this bare life he has tentatively built, there could be a
wife. There could be kids, with miniature versions of his nose
and his eyes. They would laugh and play and chatter, and it
would be fine. It could be enough. The wife wouldn't know
everything about him. Even if she suspected, she would never

ask. But she would love him, and that would be fine. It could be enough.

Or there could be nothing. He could live alone, different men and different shadows. His mother's despair, her confusion at his refusal to give her grandchildren. His father's shame, his weak, dying legs too stubborn to be supported by his disgraced son. The gossip that would permeate the village, the whispers that would kill his mother. The disappointment, their disappointment in him. In his failure.

He leans back against the bamboo chair. He has discovered that if he slides forward a little, he can still rest his neck at the top like he used to. Anamika sits behind him, more vibrant than before, with a gold band circling her dark finger.

It is raining once again, raining hard this time. Monsoon season.

'You used to say something to me,' he remembers suddenly, looking across at her. 'Every time it rained.'

She laughs, and he knows she hasn't forgotten. 'I used to ask you to dance.'

'I always said no,' he says quietly, looking out at the puddles gathering at the base of the old guava tree.

She reaches over, grabs his hand. She can do that now, however clumsy the gesture is. She is, after all, his. And he hers. 'But you finally said yes.'

There's a thought in the smell, the smell of new-rain-on-dust. A thought of purity, of change. Newness. It's a strange way to find hope, he knows. But that's the way it always is. For now, it is enough.

103

Neurons and Hormones

Thomas chooses to focus on her veins. Green and clear, they remind him of his anatomy books, of safer, smaller things. She's just blood and bone, he chides himself. Just like you. Just like you.

His problem is not new. Thomas falls in love easily and often: the pointy girl on the bus with the gold nose ring; the cashier at Big Bazaar who hands him his bananas and eggs with an especially bright-white smile; the old woman in the corner shop, who trembles as she sips tea. He has never been loved. He would like to be, he thinks. Someday. He thinks he would be good at it.

'Thomas?'

Lisa's voice, like her veins and surgical scrubs, is green. Or he imagines it would be, if he could see it. A bright, urgent green. It scares him, as does her skin, how it's so white it looks scrubbed clean. He's terrified of her beauty. He prefers to focus on her imperfections: that she carries her weight more on one side than the other, that her left eye is a little smaller than her right, that her plaits belie her origins—perfumed with Amla oil and fish fry. They calm him, just a little. Blood and bone. Neurons and hormones.

'Sorry.' He is vibrating. All over. The paper he clutches buzzes in his hand, and he clasps his wrist, willing it to stop. 'I called you here, because…' Damn. His voice is buzzing too. He clears his throat, twice, hard enough to taste bile.

Her smile reminds him of his mother's: soft and hard at the same time. Right now, it seems to mock him. He doesn't want her pity.

Two weeks ago, Thomas wrote his dreams into a letter that he never sent. Instead, per standards of propriety, he sent a more practical proposal through Suma Aunty: his fourth standard teacher, who had taught Lisa's two younger brothers and vaguely recognized her name. Suma Aunty had translated his dreams to Lisa's family, proclaiming, with much hand-on-heart hyperventilation, that Thomas was 'flat' for their daughter. (In Thomas's unsent letter, the sentiment was rendered somewhat more tenderly, but Suma had captured the gist of things.) Perhaps more was lost in translation, however, because, as Suma reported back with painful bluntness, Lisa's family was unmoved (her exact words had been: 'No chance, boy.'). Thomas was too poor, too dark, and, most damningly, too Mar Thoma (the wrong type of Christian).

Hell, what is he doing here?

No chance, boy.

Thomas knows his brain is broken—or, at the very least, bleeding. As the erstwhile captain of the All India Institute of Medical Sciences quiz team, he remembers the dates of the Cold War and the capital of Latvia. But at the moment, he doesn't seem to remember words. Or rather, he remembers too many words—they threaten to gush out of him like violence, like memory, in thick, incoherent streams—nonsense words that he can feel but can't understand—dark and blurry and far, far too much. He wants to be anyone but himself. How can he convince anyone to love him? He is so difficult to love, he has yet to master the art himself. There is still so much left to lose. He wants so much that he can hardly stand up.

Lisa's skin stretches into her skull unevenly, her hairline zigzagging into her parting. Absently, he notes that it's lucky he's only Mar Thoma, not Hindu. If she were to wear sindoor after marriage, the powder would never find a straight road home. Thomas realizes he can't remember the route of his own hairline…is that something he should know? He hates the mirror, and spends as little time in front of it as possible. But now, bizarrely, he feels compelled to know: he wants to stand in front of it, he wants to know himself. He wants to know what she sees. Does she stare at his pockmarked skin, or does she fixate on his eyes (the only part of his face he can, grudgingly, admit to favouring)? Or, the far more likely scenario—does she instead look away altogether, like he does? Option C sends a slice of quick, bright pain through his stomach.

'Because...' God, even his breath is vibrating. Shuddering.

'Thomas.' Lisa takes his hand, her watch cold and metal against his wrist. 'Let's sit down?'

Oh, thank God.

She leads him to a nearby bench, so old that splinters threaten that exposed swath of ankle. 'You want to talk to me about the proposal, yes?'

He nods. His mouth is brittle-dry.

'Well, as you know, my parents oppose.'

Again.

'Because you're Mar Thoma, and we're Catholic. But I don't care about those things.'

'You don't?' Ah, there was his voice, staticky though it may be. His heart is beating too fast. His breath is coming too fast. Malayalam feels odd in his mouth, so sticky, so much tongue. All those palatals and glottals. After years in the North, he has forgotten how coarse his mother tongue sounds, how harsh it is in the bright white of the hospital.

She shakes her head so thoroughly that tiny curls of hair at her temple quake. 'I only care that my husband be kind. And clever.' Her white skin flushes, and Thomas watches the blood rush to her cheeks with genuine scientific curiosity; he is too dark to blush. 'And you are.'

'I am?'

'Yes.'

A brief, tense pause, during which Thomas almost forgets she'd taken his hand, until she squeezes it, rippling the silence.

'Are you...' He stops, swallows. Twice. 'You're...'

'Yes.' Her fingers are warm on his; their thighs curve into each other. 'I'm saying I'll marry you.'

Something lodges in his chest, something heavy and tight. He kisses her, immediately, clumsily, before she gets the chance to realize just how much she has lost. He feels like he's tricked her. Tricked himself. Tricked fate. He can't believe he's won.

Four months later, they are married.

Later, much later, at a dinner party thousands of miles away from Trivandrum Medical College, Lisa will recount this story and laugh and laugh. 'I proposed to myself!' she'll say. 'No, actually, I talked myself into proposing to myself!' And Thomas will smile indulgently and wait, still, for the reckoning that has not yet come.

Butter Chicken

Houston in July smells like India. Smoke, earth, rain. Trash. Geckos stare at Beena from crannies in the porch. At night, the hard exoskeletons of beetles litter the patio just like they do back home, burst open like ripe mangoes under the sun.

The church itself smells of wet perfume and people. Too many people. All different shades of brown, Beena the lightest. Bhavna sits beside her, itching in her ruffles. She had spent the hour before leaving complaining that her churidar top was too tight, her churidar pants too long, her face too chalky with Johnson & Johnson baby powder. Beena dragged the comb through her daughter's hair, pausing every few seconds when it got stuck in curly brambles, and told her to shut up. The bishop was coming today, and, although they'd shed religion long ago, it was necessary to perform piety for the sake of the pictures that would inevitably be WhatsApped to India.

In the end, they'd ended up leaving late in sulky silence. Malayalees had filled the church to capacity, so they leaned against the walls, feet aching, backs cramping. They only saw the bishop through the blurry zoom of an old camera lens, his face pixelated and grotesque. WhatsApp-worthy. The sermon itself is torpid, focussed on Mary's purity and piety. Even the bishop seems bored, swinging incense as if in search of something to fill the time.

The last time Beena had given any thought to Mary was when she was giving birth to Bhavna, almost fourteen years ago. When her voice was thick and Indian, and her bones visible in her wrists. When she was overwhelmed with dampness. In her brain, between her breasts, between her legs. Wetness she has come to associate with womanhood. The labour room had been private, throbbing with stale, cool air. She'd wondered—absently, because sleep was tugging at her mind—why her body felt like an evacuation site. The drugs hadn't fully worn off yet; they buzzed bluely around her, within her, filling her head with half-formed images. Most prominent among them was Mary, Mary mother of God as she was in Nativity scenes played out in white porcelain: Mary, Joseph, the three wise men. Baby Jesus in the manger.

Even as a child, Beena had studied Mary's serene statue and wondered how, just hours earlier, she could have been crying out on the floor of the barn, a small god pressing on her uterus, damp with the same womanly wetness that Beena felt then. This, more than her mother's advice before her contractions quickened, was what soothed her on the day of her daughter's birth. That Mary—that hallowed figure she had not thought of in years, not since she and her family shed their religion like snakes shed skins—once crouched on all fours amid straw and dung, her cervix dilating like everyone else's, her baby god pink and slimy like everyone else's. Her body ordinary and girlish, bent in pain—human pain, the pain of everyday miracles. There was something unholy and precious about this image of Mary, weeping not for her child or what he would do, but for herself, for her smallness, her humanness and her pain.

There was a comfort in this, this feeling that something that happened to her, in her, was ancient and precious and holy. Comfort *Sugham* in Malayalam, a word used for anything and everything. Anil once made a face at a cup of tea Beena made for him, saying, 'Oru sugham illa.' Translated literally: there is no comfort in this cup of tea. How quaint, that a cup of tea could—or should—bring comfort. But isn't that what it does?

Bhavna would grow up speaking crisply and crassly, like an American. The little Malayalam she knew would always be mixed with English. They called it Manglish, this mixing, and to Beena the name was apt: it sounded horrific, like mangling, mauling. Like something broken. For as long as Beena could remember, there was Indian and there was American. But now there was an entirely new hybrid to cage and categorize, a monster with tiger teeth and an eagle's beak. A baby who spat out dal but ate mush from glass bottles labelled 'pureed peas.'

There was a foreign familiarity about their dynamic, this mother and daughter, strangers who had once shared a body. At times, Bhavna would suckle at Beena's breasts until they were red and raw and chapped, smiling a smile that terrified Beena. Smiling as though, despite her helplessness and her hunger, she recognized her superiority. Perhaps this, not what the doctors told her about her fertility, was why she never had any other children. Even as she loved the child of her creation, Beena never forgot to keep her at an arm's length.

It was clear, early on, that Bhavna had inherited Anil's looks. Beena was a beauty, or had been, anyway: milk skin, hazel eyes. Her hair swung behind her in a tight, thick plait; her eyebrows arched without tweezing, a small beauty-mark dotted in between them like a permanent bindi. She had been pined for and sought after, receiving the biodata of boys from cities as far away as Pune. She accepted Anil because he promised her America. Anil, unlike the others, was reserved. He had a high brow and a low paunch. He didn't woo her; he barely even spoke to her. The marriage was arranged through their parents, and accepted, tepidly, by its participants.

Bhavna was born fair, but turned dark and patchy with childhood eczema. As a baby, her softness and roundness had been praised. At ten, Beena's circle tutted about it, offering Beena quiet advice about healthy recipes and the importance of exercise. Her hair remained a mystery to her mother, so thick and unmanageable that it routinely broke combs before succumbing to coconut oil. Once, on a trip back home to

Trivandrum, Anil had confessed quietly that he felt guilty for Bhavna's appearance. He'd married a gold medal, and diluted her genes, he said. They'd produced a bronze. The words tightened into a seed at the pit of Beena's stomach. A talkative child, Bhavna closed in on herself as she grew. There was a muchness to her, a steady and secret padding of layers. Beena does not understand her daughter. Worse, she doesn't know if she wants to.

Beena has almost dozed off when the bishop finally stops droning. Communion is taken—not by them, of course—peace is exchanged, and the Mallus migrate to an attached banquet hall. Sitting there, under broken fans in the heavy humidity, Beena is ambushed by Anu.

Anu had gone to medical school with Beena's father's brother's wife's sister. In America, that made them family. She had lived in Texas for over twenty years, and there was no doubt in anyone's mind that, whatever the American Dream meant, Anu Aunty had attained it. Her children were grown now, one studying biology at Yale, the other computer science at Carnegie Mellon. Her husband is a chiropractor with his own practice. She, trained in dermatology, owns a 'wellness clinic' that specializes in sucking the blood out of cheeks, spinning it and re-injecting it. Although she must be at least a decade older than Beena, she looks younger and shinier, her skin bright under her eyes and tight at her temple.

They make small talk about enrolling Bhavna in a good high school, because 'it all starts there, you know,' about

Beena's interest in starting a garden. Anu claps her hands here, exclaiming, 'Oh! I'm so glad you're keeping busy!' Beena's eyes twitch, but she says nothing. Anu shifts her attention to Bhavna. She grasps her chin, turning it one way and then the other, as though she is admiring something sparkly.

'Bhavna kutty,' she says, and it takes Beena Herculean strength to force her eyes not to roll, 'it's such a pity, you've become so dark. You know, when you were a baby, you were so fair and pretty.'

'Mm,' Bhavna mumbles. Beena winces when she sees Anu's French manicured nails digging into her daughter's jaw, leaving red crescent clefts in their wake. She smells strongly of lavender, of something violet and violent.

'You know, I may have just the thing for you,' Anu continues. 'We use it all the time at the clinic and it works wonders on dark complexions. Take a ripe tomato, mash it, mix it with a few drops of lemon juice—'

'Add chicken,' Bhavna interrupts. 'Marinate and cook for thirty minutes. Enjoy!'

Anu lets go of Bhavna's chin. Her eyes are wide, mascara-clumpy lashes fluttering in shock.

Around the purple-clothed table, Beena sees faces go as red as brown skin could. Anil's lips are set in a tight line, and Beena can tell that he is grinding his teeth together, wearing away at enamel against the dentist's warnings. Beena knows, by now, that he does this when stifling giggles.

'What?' Bhavna asks. Her voice is high and holds only the

hint of a quiver. 'Aren't you making butter chicken?'

'Anu,' Beena finally says, gathering herself enough to form the words. 'We're so sorry. Bhavna had a long day, and she's just tired. She meant no offence.'

Anu Aunty rolls her shoulders in, sticks her chin up. 'Of course. None taken.'

Beena feels as though she's just run a marathon. She can't stop shaking. She stares at her daughter, mouth agape, proud and scared of her, of this ferocious girl she'd grown herself. She is, after all, a person that Beena does not know. In this knowledge, there is a certain sugham.

Family History

By the time Riya is diagnosed with bipolar disorder type II, she is sixteen and unsurprised.

When she was eight years old, she wandered downstairs at night for water and instead found her couch on fire. Her father, eyes lit orange and red, demonic against the night, fanned the flames quietly by jabbing toothpicks into the cushions, one by one. He did it so methodically, solemnly, with a twist in his mouth that suggested a chore. Riya tried to scream—not for help, but to help; she didn't yet believe her father was crazy—but the sound lodged in her throat, tangled somewhere between marrow and smoke. Months later, long after the scream was let out, heard and answered, the smoke-stench remained in her living room, seeping out of the singed carpets and coiling around the feet of the brand-new sofa.

Now, she sits in a hospital room, listening to the news that seems both staggering and inevitable. She's known Dr Patel all her life. He delivered her older sister, who is now eighteen.

He cried when her youngest brother died after several days in the neonatal intensive care unit, his tiny lungs swelling and deflating like ripped balloons. He counselled her mother through suicide attempts and panic attacks. He assured her that, although the baby was born prematurely because her husband punched her stomach during one of his outbursts, her son's death was in no way her fault. In a lot of ways, Dr Patel knows Riya better than her best friends. So, when he clears his throat and talks about her family history of bipolar disorder, she knows exactly what's coming.

'It's nothing to be ashamed of, Riya,' Dr Patel says, after a long pause in which Riya pretends to find her chipped nail polish endlessly fascinating. 'It's something that a lot of people struggle with, and it typically manifests in people your age—especially in creative, high-achieving people. There's a genetic component, too—you know that your mother struggles with depression and your father, well...' He waits, as though hoping for a response. Receiving none, he sighs and continues, 'The good news is that now that we know what's going on, we can start treatment and you'll feel better.'

Riya nods. There's a familiar urge to scream building up in her throat. Sometimes, it gets so strong she feels as though she might disintegrate. But today, it settles like a rock in her stomach. She thinks about asking the question. *The* question, the one that's haunted her since her childhood. *Am I crazy?*

Because there's always been that fear. Ever since her father was hauled away by police after leaving red thumbprints around her mother's neck that didn't fade for weeks, there's been that fear. That voice telling her that maybe she got more from him than coarse black hair and a love of spicy food.

Dr Patel's eyebrows are thicker than any she's seen before, with little black-and-grey hairs tickling the rims of his bifocals. Right now, they're pushed into one misshapen line bent in the middle with concern. 'Riya, I can keep talking—you know I love to talk your ear off—but I think we should discuss this, together. What are you thinking?'

Riya scrapes a flake of red nail polish from her thumb. It comes off perfectly, in one whole piece that she rolls up into a rubbery spiral. It satisfies her, this perfect peel. 'Am I crazy, Dr Patel?' She refuses to look into his eyes.

'Ahem, well—' he coughs, clears his throat again, one too many times. 'That's not a label we'd ever use, Riya. There's no such thing as crazy, or as normal, even. There's just you, and what's going on in your brain.'

'Bullshit.' Riya sits up in her chair, uncrossing her leg so that her foot hits the carpet with a quiet thud. 'That's bullshit and you know it.'

This time, it's Dr Patel who can't seem to meet her eyes. His hands meet over his domed stomach, fiddling with a stray fraying button. 'Listen, I know this must come as a shock—'

'No, it fucking doesn't.' Riya crushes the flake of nail polish between her thumb and forefinger, spitting the words out before they are fully formed in her mind. It's out of character for her, and she can't grasp why she's reacting this way when she knew. She's known. She's always known. Ever since she spent the night after the fire painting her room, the living room, and half of the kitchen a disastrous shade of crusty beige she found in the garage. She was eight. She'd fallen asleep clutching the paint roller to her chest, her head resting on the ladder in a way that would leave an imprint in the morning, hungrily breathing in paint fumes to rid herself of the smell of smoke.

There's not much more to say. Dr Patel assures her once again that she is not crazy, just unwell, and that with the proper treatment—a combination of new antipsychotic drugs and the traditional lithium pills—she'll feel like herself in no time.

He has no idea. She can't imagine what that would be like, to feel like herself. She doesn't know what 'herself' feels like.

The weather outside is a sticky middle ground between cold and hot, so Riya alternates between unzipping and zipping her jacket as she walks towards the car. Newly-minted license in hand, she'd been so proud to tell her mother that she could drive herself to this doctor's appointment. No need for her to worry, it was just a routine check-up, and she had a piece of plastic certifying her more than capable of turning a wheel. Just before she headed out the door, her older sister Sanjana stopped her, snatched the keys out of her hand.

'Where do you think you're going, stupid?' Sanjana teased,

that characteristically smug smile tugging at her mouth. 'Come on, I'll drive you. I need to meet Lisa at the library anyway.'

'No, don't worry about it,' Riya muttered, her fingers itching to grab the keys that her sister held high over her head to taunt her. 'I told Amma I'd drive. It'll be good practice for me.'

'Save your practice. Unlike you, I actually need the car,' her sister retorted, and her voice, still gentle, carried that tone of finality that rendered her the family authority in their father's absence. 'I'll drive you wherever you need to go, don't worry.' Sanjana lowered her hand to carelessly pat Riya's shoulder, that archaic remnant of a childhood they'd never really had, and that was all it took.

'God-fucking-damnit, I'm not a baby!' Riya pushed Sanjana's hand away, grabbing the keys so roughly they cut thin red tracks on her sister's palms. 'Don't pretend you're doing me a fucking favour by driving when I know you're just dying to go make out with your pothead boyfriend behind McDonald's. Oh wait, sorry, I forgot—you're going to the library? With Lisa? With all the studying you do these days, it's a miracle you're still failing calculus.'

Her chest heaved up and down, but nothing about the silence that followed made Riya feel like she'd won. Ears ringing, hands trembling, she pointedly ignored the tears drawing mascara rivers down Sanjana's cheeks, and strode purposefully, albeit somewhat shakily, to the door.

'You know, you're just like Dad,' Sanjana said before she

could leave. Her tone was soft, but the words make Riya's heartbeat slow and her vision blur. She turned around in slow motion, preparing to yell that no, she's not like Dad, not even a little bit like Dad, she couldn't be like Dad, because she's not a psycho. She's not evil. But the words didn't come. She thought she might be crying tearlessly, soundlessly, because her mouth gaped wide open but she couldn't seem to swallow enough air to breathe.

Now, Riya stares at the car in the almost-empty parking lot. A silver Prius, glowing an ethereal blue under the Texas sun, parked terribly—although she'd been happy with herself for getting it within the white lines earlier. It's mocking her. She drops the keys somewhere on the ground—or at least, she assumes she does. She can't really remember. She starts to run.

Naale

'Chaaya, chaaya, chaaye, kaapi, kaapi, kaapi!'

The vendors' cries vibrate in the train compartment. Outside the glassless windows, it's a stifling January afternoon, the humidity soggy with sweat and urine. Too hot for the vendors' steaming tea and coffee; too bright to look up into the sun. Throngs of commuters, their eyebrows furrowed, cheekbones caked with city smut, pour into the train relentlessly, filling every spare seat. They leave behind dusty footprints as they travel the same route they have walked a thousand times.

A girl, not quite seventeen, sits in the corner of the compartment. Eyes lined with kajal, lips lined with rouge, her face is painted to perfection. A modest shawl shrouds her tightly-pinned hair; an array of bangles bite into her hennaed wrists, placed primly in her lap. The archetypal young bride, she sits across from her new husband, a man with large glasses and a small suitcase. He is buried in a newspaper that flaps across his face, but she, wide-eyed, is craning her head to see as far as she can beyond the bars of the window. Whenever a puff of smoke wafts into her face, she scrunches her eyes shut and giggles. Despite having left her home, her family and her life behind to marry a stranger she's only met once before, the girl is thrilled, above all, by the prospect of finally riding a train.

With a lurch, the train begins to creep forward, crawling out of the station, hurtling her into a new life. The view beyond the bars starts to shift as the train cuts through lush, tropical Kerala, moving north. As the familiar lanes of her childhood pass by, the girl is struck by a sudden fear. She wishes she could slow time; she wishes she could freeze this moment, this delight of riding a train, before it crawls to a stop in Bhilai, the place she must learn to call home.

The passengers settle, the dust rises. As day slips into night, a lull settles over the compartment; one by one, everyone drifts into sleep. The girl, Cecily, leans her head against the rubber seat back. Her eyes threaten to close, but she blinks quickly, once, then twice, shaking the sleep off. The chaos of the wedding day and her travels kept her suspended in adrenaline for two days; now, exhaustion sticks to her like the static in her dupatta. Fidgeting to stay awake and take in the first moments of her second life, her restless gaze bounces from the window to the man sitting across from her. Her husband. The person with whom she will spend the rest of her life. The stranger with whom, after the traditional whirlwind engagement and marriage, she has yet to have a proper conversation. Her smile fades.

He is still reading, squinting in the dying light, a pair of oversized spectacles perched on his hooked nose. Feeling her scrutiny, he looks up and gives her a slight nod of acknowledgment. He's a dignified man, ten years her senior, with penetrating eyes and a high brow—a sign of intellect, her mother always said. A good man, her father had told her. A good match.

She has no way of knowing what the future holds, except that he is it. He is her future.

How is it, she wonders, that yesterday she was a child, and today, a wife? Just three months ago, she had been taking care of her three nieces when her sister came to her with news of a proposal. Her nieces were three little devils, younger than her by only six years, each with identical puffs of coarse hair and wide eyes that glint with mischief. They always felt closer to her than her older sister, who had been married off when Cecily was only ten years old. That day, the triplets engrossed her in a make-believe game, in which she was a witch and they were wizards, bent on defeating her. She had been laughing with them, yelling at them, drawing in the dust with sticks snapped from the branches of a teak tree, when her older sister had rushed outside. Her usually-smooth bun frizzed; her sari fluttered in the dirt behind her. That was how Cecily had known something was different. Something was wrong. 'Get up, quickly.' Her sister's voice was different, too. Jagged, somehow. 'You have guests. Go, serve the chaaya.'

Cecily, confused but obedient, had shaken loose soil from her skirt, and dutifully poured three cups of masala tea with a hand she willed not to shake for the strange family in her living room.

That was that, and a wedding was planned before she knew where she was. She remembers the time between the engagement and marriage as she would a dream—just a blur of noise and colour. On the day of the wedding, she whispered to her mother that, for the first time, she felt like an adult. Growing up as the youngest in a family of seven boys and six girls, she had always been a child, the pampered baby of the house. Now, all eyes were on her. In her new silk sari, ornamented with heavy jewellery—jhumka earrings, a gold-plated necklace, and a thin golden band—she felt beautiful. She felt grown.

'Not just an adult,' her mother had responded. 'A wife.'

The band seems to burn on her finger. She fidgets with it, twisting it this way and that. Increasingly agitated, she stares at this ring, this tiny thing that has taken over her life, that will control her future, as another hand covers hers. Darker, larger. Decorated with its own matching gold band. She looks up, taken aback, to see her new husband smile at her for the first time.

'What are you thinking about?' His voice is soft.

She stammers. About the future, she says. About their life. About how she doesn't know how to cook, and she doesn't know where to learn. Are there books? Maybe her mother-in-law would teach her? Maybe—

'When I get overwhelmed with worries about the future,' he says, curbing her thoughts before they tripped over each other, 'do you know what I do?' She shakes her head; he smiles again. 'I go to sleep. And deal with it tomorrow.' She starts to protest, but he squeezes her hand. 'Naale.'

Like a spell, his words conjure sleep immediately. Her body fills with a sudden, startling warmth. As her eyes close and the world fogs, the last image in her mind is their two linked hands, their two glinting rings. The bands—shiny, brand new, and filled with possibilities—glow with the promise of tomorrow. For the first time, the prospect doesn't scare her.

Naale.

Author's Note: *Thank you, Ammachy, for inspiring this story.*

It Dreamt Itself Away

Sometimes, he dreams as babies do—or at least, how he imagines they do. In curls and twists and whirls, in fading colours and soft musical hums. That's what it must be, right? What keeps a baby so content when it's dreaming?

This is what Sapan thinks of now, as he leans over the glass edge of the hospital's newborn cot. His sister is one of the many babies in this room. He'd been startled when he walked in, never having seen so many babies in one place before. It is a sea of pink-blue blankets and hats with fuzzy bobbles—but he would've recognized his sister even if his father hadn't pointed her out immediately. Not because she has his grandfather's nose, as his mother murmured happily, or his Ada Aunty's cheeks, as his father muttered less happily, but because she is the only brown baby in the room of red and pink babies.

His sister is new, brand-new, just-born, fragile like his brand-new train set, but she already looks old. Older than him by far, and he has a good six years on her. Her cheeks are wrinkly, deep lines running down from her nose to her mouth, frozen bird-formations just above her barely-there eyebrows. When he saw her before, swaddled in his mother's sagging arms, she was crying—the petulant, whiny cry of the stray cat living on their fence in India, the one his mother always warned him to be wary of because it could be sick. Now, in slumber, she looks happy for the first time in her short life. She sighs deeply and serenely, like an old man, and paws at her face with a tiny pink hand. He even thinks he sees her smile, although his father is quick to tell him that it's not a true smile yet, just instinct. He grins when she twitches her index finger, curls her hand into a fist, and keeps on dreaming. She's a person called Sanjana, and they share dreams.

He knows that she is smiling, even if his father doesn't think so.

⌾

Other times, he dreams in film noir, like the movies he's recently come to love. Guys in suspenders and undone ties, surrounded by coils of cigar smoke. Girls with coiffed hair and bright red lipstick—you can tell it's red even through the black-and-white.

He likes to pretend he's in one of those movies, and, in his apartment, it isn't hard to do. There's not much colour around. The carpet is beige—used to be white, his mother frequently scolds—and the walls are cream to match. Even the window faces the peeling grey walls of the neighbouring apartment complex, nothing else. His mother hates it. When his father isn't around, she tells him how much she hates the dreary wall colour, the broken-not-broken television. How she wishes the place belonged to them and not the grumpy landlord downstairs, so she could paint it a shade of mint-green she found in *Home and Design*.

Then again, his mother hates mostly everything. Sometimes, he thinks this includes his father. She serves him dinner in silence, usually much later than when they eat, because his father only comes home around eight. She brings him tea before brewing her own, every morning at six-thirty, just when Sapan is brushing his teeth in his Mario Kart pajamas. But he doesn't ever say thank you, and she looks away. They don't hug or kiss in front of him like his friends' parents do—one time, after second-grade graduation, he saw Timothy's parents kiss and then smile at each other like the actors in his movies. It made him feel odd, knowing that people, that parents, do that in real life. Once, while he was sitting in the backseat of the car on their way to a function at Aditya Uncle's house, he thought he saw his father putting his arm around his mother's shoulders. But it turned out that he was just getting ready to reverse.

His mother met Vijay Uncle at the Indian grocer's two blocks down from their apartment. At least that is what she tells him when he comes home from school on Tuesday after Robotics Club, and there is a man he's never seen before sitting on his sofa, smoking a cigarette.

'Sapan, this is Vijay Uncle. He just moved here from India and lives very close to us, a few houses down,' his mother says. Her face is flushed, her lips are coated in red, and she's wearing the expensive perfume his father bought her for their fifteenth wedding anniversary four months ago, the one she only wears for special occasions.

He smiles, says hello, goes to his room to do his homework and play video games. By now, he is used to the parade of Indians his parents befriend. The pot-bellied uncles who start the evening with their mouths settled in tight lines, but end up singing old Hindi love songs in a drunken bliss. The gossiping aunties who sit around the kitchen in saris that don't move as they do, talking about Cousin Indu, who eloped with an American, and her poor family who must be so upset about it that they couldn't come to this gathering. And of course, the continuing annoyance of their limitless children, who they lug around to every event and whose wellbeing will inevitably become Sapan's responsibility, as the forever-oldest child.

But Vijay Uncle is different. He carries with him no wife, no children, no potbelly. He seems relaxed, at ease with himself when he talks to Sapan's mother, and doesn't recognize that he's unwanted when Sapan's father merely nods to acknowledge his presence. He smokes cigarettes and keeps his mustache trim, his cuffs rolled up, and his tie loosened, although he never takes it off.

He notes Vijay Uncle's difference, his peculiarity against the sameness of their lives, but he doesn't think much of it. Doesn't care much about it. He has a ten-page report on Russia's tsars due next Monday for his ninth-grade World History class, so he goes upstairs and puts on his headphones.

Sapan stores the uncomfortable visits in the back of his head, saying a curt hello and disappearing to his room when he sees him again on Wednesday and once again on Thursday. He ignores the disconcerting scent of his mother's Safrant Troublant perfume mingled with the dry cigarette-smell lingering in the living room one Saturday morning when his father was on-call at the hospital and didn't come home at all.

He asks no questions, just as his father, who sits in his armchair and notices an unfamiliar dent in its cushions, who goes to the bathroom and finds stubs in the trash can, who can smell samosas frying in his sleep but acts oblivious to the smoke-stench that clouds their living room, asks no questions.

Later Sapan will think back on this time in his life and realize that, had it been anyone but his mother, he would have known it was an affair.

After the visits stop, his mother grows quiet. Her lipstick lies unused by his parents' sink, eventually growing old enough to throw out. The infamous perfume, purchased by one man and used for another, sits forgotten in her vanity cupboard. She stops going out to their numerous Indian functions, claiming to have a stomachache, a headache, a fever. Sometimes, in the middle of the night, when he's out getting a glass of water or using the bathroom, he sees her sitting at the kitchen table, staring at fruit-flies swarming overripe bananas.

Some weeks later, in the middle of dinner, she suddenly announces that she's booked a trip to India. They all tip their heads up and stare at her with hands suspended halfway between mouths and plates.

Sanjana is the first to snap out of the shock. She begins wailing, says, 'Mommy, I can't miss school, plus I have Jessica's birthday party on Saturday, and she's turning nine, it's important!'

Sapan soon joins her: 'Mom, are you serious? You know I have exams coming up—'

His father is alone in his stillness, staring hard at Sapan's mother as if he's willing the next words out of her mouth. She complies, waving a hand as if to brush away their complaints. 'No,' she clarifies, speaking as though she may stumble over her words, 'the trip is for me.'

She goes on to explain how her father is sick and how it is important for her to spend some time with him, caring for him in his old age. Sapan finds it odd that she chooses now to go, considering his grandfather had a mild heart attack a year ago and has since recovered, according to the doctors. She's leaving in a month, will be gone for four. 'At least,' she adds, in case anyone is confused.

He doesn't say anything, nobody does. His father looks down intently at his meal. Sanjana is still crying. Sapan carefully rolls a ball of rice in his fingers and puts it in his mouth. The chicken, he notes, is especially spicy today.

Since his father works late hours, it is decided that it will be best if the children move in with Ada Aunty and Aditya Uncle for a little while. After all, Sanjana is only eight and can't possibly be expected to take care of herself when Sapan goes to a friend's house or an overnight competition. Their home is only a few miles away; there is no need to even transfer schools. It seems like the perfect set-up until his mother comes back.

Ada Aunty has a round, pleasant face and an inviting smile. Her house, much nicer than their cramped apartment, is often the designated meeting-place for their parents' crowd of Indian friends. Unlike his mother, who long ago shed her traditional clothes in favour of casual western outfits, Ada Aunty still wears ironed saris in the daytime and ragged cotton ones at night.

Aditya Uncle is friendly as well, with bushy eyebrows and a wide mouth. He is an accountant, and is always home at five sharp. Sapan wishes his father had a job like that sometimes, instead of one where he rushes out of the house at two in the morning trying to save a stranger's life.

After school, there are always snacks on the coffee-table. Crackers and cheese, usually, but since Sanjana mentioned that they love Nutella, there's often a chocolate-spread sandwich as well. Ada Aunty never hogs the television like their mother. Instead, she cooks elaborate dinners and, if she has time left, she cleans. She cleans every inch of the house, the places nobody but only she knows about: the crevice behind the mantle, the cracked floorboard underneath the Persian rug. She cleans until everything sparkles, until her hands are blistered. Sapan has heard the women gossiping about Ada Aunty; how she insisted on finishing college before searching for a husband, how her father had to pay a lot of money for Aditya Uncle to marry her because she was dark and homely. Now, watching her furiously scrub dried curry out of a dinner plate, he wonders what her college major was. He wonders whether she wishes that her life was different.

Then, one day, he knows that she does. That day, Aditya Uncle doesn't come home until nine at night. He's drunk. His face is shiny-red, and he is angrier than Sapan has ever seen him. Ada Aunty tells him and Sanjana to go to bed early, and they do, but he lies awake, listening to their voices rise and fall deep into the blackness. The next morning, there is a bruise high up on Ada Aunty's cheekbone, right where her skin stretches into her temple.

It happens again, a few weeks later, and again, a few months later. The four months that his mother speculated earlier have turned into five, six. He notices a pattern: it's usually on Saturdays, and it's always when he's drunk. Sapan has never seen him hit her, but he sees things that are not in the spots they normally are the next day, the spots that Ada Aunty has designated for them.

Boots, books, belts.

Anything.

They pick up Sapan's mother at the airport, seven months after she left. She's different. She wears bright colours and laughs loudly. Her hair is streaked with henna. She runs towards them, knocking over Sanjana's homemade 'Welcome home, Amma!' sign. She hugs them tightly, so tightly it almost overshadows the fact that she doesn't hug their father at all. As she straightens her back, he pats her shoulder. She flinches, but places her hand over his, so briefly Sapan almost misses it.

There was a time when this would have given him some glimmer of comfort. But he's older now—old enough to diagnose the touch: cold, clinical. Obligatory intimacy.

He becomes a doctor, of course. There was never really any other choice. At his graduation, his mother cheers the loudest, his father beams proudly. The picture Sanjana took that day shows the three of them squinting at the sunlight and smiling the same crooked smile.

Gayatri is the first and the last girl he meets. His parents are so glad he hasn't married an American, like Sanjana, that they don't pressure him to meet more. Over tea, he learns that she is an art history major, an accomplished kathak dancer and a decent singer. She doesn't offer up this information, of course. Her mother, a bird-like, hyperactive woman with a shrill voice and arms that remind him of talons, is all too eager to feed it to him, along with the plate of orange laddoos she claims Gayatri made herself.

Still, there's something he likes about her. Maybe it's that she's an art history major, not a doctor or an engineer. Maybe it's the way she juts out her chin, even while looking down demurely. Anyway, he marries her. What else is he supposed to do?

They met at a bar, of course. Where else? She ordered vodka, he asked for scotch. She pulled her seat closer and didn't need to do anything more. They walked to the car. He tugged off her jacket. He noticed her wedding ring glittering on her fourth finger and became vaguely aware of the dull gold band around his own. What was proper in such situations? Should he take it off, or attempt to hide it? Did she care? Did he?

As he lies awake that night, for a brief stutter in time, the thought crosses his mind that such deception is wrong, that what he is doing is wrong. But sleep comes to him softly, and, as is the case with many such silly thoughts, it dreamt itself away.

Shaadi.com

Sheba Thomas:

Education: Delhi University, B.A.
Biography: Modern, educated woman seeking a life partner.
Caste, religion, and skin colour no bar.
Appearance: Slim build, wheatish complexion.

George Mathai:

Education: University of Texas—Houston, M.D.
Biography: U.S. based doctor seeking a fair, English-speaking,
Syrian Christian woman.
Appearance: Fair, athletic.

The pennukaanal—'bride-viewing'—is arranged by the boy's side, who consider the girl a catch, and accepted by the girl's side, who consider America a catch.

The girl's side lives in the rich part of town. The boy's side tuts about how tacky they are, clearly from new money, when they get out of the car, but as they greet the girl's side, they congratulate them on their lovely home. The girl's side smiles and waves the boy's side in, muttering to each other how the boy is not quite as 'athletic' as his biodata made him out to be. America must not be the land of George Clooneys they'd envisioned.

The boy's side sits, squished, on a divan that is not supposed to seat six people. They drink tea out of the girl-side's best china. They compliment the girl's mother on her cutlet-making skills; she brushes off the compliments and insists that it was all the girl. Although she is quite educated, the girl's mother stresses, she is still a very good homemaker. In addition to chicken cutlets, the girl makes the best fish curry the girl's side has ever tasted. Better than any hotel.

The boy's side smiles and shifts uncomfortably in their seats. The small talk becomes stifling. Finally, the girl walks in. The boy's side murmurs greetings and scrutinizes her. Decent-looking, although it was a pity about her nose and her hair, and it was quite plain that she would gain weight after a child or two. But overall not bad. And the fish curry would be a bonus.

The boy's side asks easy questions at first. Where does the girl work? Does she enjoy her work? Why did she go to college in Delhi? Then the questions get more pressing. Does she want to keep working? If so, how will she balance work and children? How many children?

The girl's side is graceful. The girl's mother provides answers the girl cannot, or does not want to. When the room gets too hot, the girl's side suggests that the girl and the boy talk in private. The boy and the girl agree immediately, and, when they step outside, the two sides congratulate each other on their matchmaking skills. How good they look together! What beautiful children they'll have!

When they run out of small talk, the two sides cross and uncross their legs. The boy's side says, again, how beautiful the house is. The girl's side says, again, thank you. It was built almost a century ago, by the girl's great-great-grandfather. The girl's mother pulls out an old photo album to 1) brag about their family wealth (and, in doing so, prove the boy-side's hypothesis about new money wrong) and 2) pass the time, which seemed to be defying the laws of physics in its sluggishness.

The boy's side perfunctorily marvels over the old photos in the album, tapping their legs against the divan and slurping back the dregs remaining in their cups. What could the boy and girl possibly be talking about for so long?

The murmurs had just started when the boy and girl walk back in, both red-faced. How did it go? The sides ask immediately, hungrily. Blank-faced, the boy and girl look at each other for confirmation. Well, it went well, they say at the same time. Everyone cheers, patting the boy's back and pinching the girl's cheeks. Time to plan another visit, the boy's side says. This time, the girl's side must come over to their home. After all, they also have quite a nice house. The girl's side smiles and agrees, promising to call soon.

As the boy's side is ushered out the door, the girl's mother notices one of the small cousins on the boy's side still playing with the photo album. Come on, mon, the girl's mother says. Time to get going. You'll come back soon, I'm sure.

The small cousin picks up the album and points to a picture. Look, he says, in a clear, high voice. It's Mariamma Aunty!

The boy's side laughs. Of course it's not Mariamma Aunty, they say. Mariamma Aunty died last year, estranged from the family after eloping with an undesirable. It must just be someone who looks like her.

But the girl's side is not laughing. Their mouths are open, eyes wide. Because Mariamma Aunty was not just the boy's great-aunt. She was also the wife of the girl's great-uncle.

Silence.

Shuffling.

Well! An uncle on the boy's side coughs. So this is off, then, is it? He is shushed, quite violently, on both sides. But his comment stirs the silence, and both sides allow themselves to laugh. What a misunderstanding! How could they not have known? Of course, you never can know all these things, after all. Thank goodness they'd caught it in time, that's all. They'd dodged a bullet. They laugh and laugh and laugh and, finally, horrified, embarrassed, and more than a little relieved, the boy's side and the girl's side part ways.

Hyphenated

The baby was born five pounds six ounces, dark-eyed, curly-haired, and dead.

Although the doctors tried valiantly to explain why, Neal could never quite wrap his head around it. Something about placental abruption. No fault of theirs, of course…and all signs indicated that Nikki would have no trouble having children in the future, if they so chose.

The world blurred. Both heightened and blunted. Neal doesn't remember the colour of the hospital walls or sheets, but he can't forget the metallic pallor of his wife's throat, the red veins crisscrossing the skin of her still-bulging stomach. He can't, try as he might, forget holding his dead son against his chest—gingerly, like someone might hold an acquaintance's child with a full diaper. Whenever he catches a glimpse of the picture they took that day, a morbid souvenir forced upon them by a nurse intent on making the process as 'comfortable' as possible for them, he feels as though he's looking into the broken shards of a mirror. At a man trying desperately to disguise a grimace as a smile, holding one lifeless body, hugging another with all the life drained out of her. A man masquerading as him, but not quite succeeding at the hoax.

Now, watching Nikki bustle around the room, packing her suitcase with quick, nimble movements, he shakes his head. Pushes the image of distorted fatherhood out of his mind. *You don't belong here, Suraj.* 'Sun' in Hindi. They'd bickered over it for weeks, but finally settled on Suraj for a boy, Chanda—'moon'—for a girl. Both sun and moon had set now, leaving behind a darkness as deep and wide as the abyss between them.

'Have you seen my charger?' Nikki asks, not looking up from the dupatta she's folding into impossibly small sections. 'I can't find it anywhere.'

Neal fumbles behind their nightstand, pulls out a white tangled cord fraying at the ends. 'You can't use it there without an adaptor, though.'

'Shit, you're right.' She pauses, biting her bottom lip, that new faraway look crawling into her eyes. 'It's been so long, I'd forgotten.' Her lipstick is dry and peeling, and her recent refusal to look in the mirror while applying makeup has given her a strange, crimson shadow of a second lip. A lopsided, painted smile.

When they first met, back when she was still calling herself 'Nilakshi' and spoke with a musical Carnatic lilt, her lips were one of the first things he noticed about her: full and bowed

148

and always curved into a smile. That first day, a lifetime ago, when she bumped into him at a friend-of-a-friend's party and spilled tamarind chutney down his shirt.

'I'm so sorry!' she had exclaimed, biting her bottom lip.

The anger fizzing in his chest stopped when he met her gaze. While she wasn't traditionally beautiful, those eyes—such a dark, dark, luminous brown, almost black. Those eyes and those lips and that one dimple. He thought he'd fallen in love on the spot.

On their honeymoon, he mentioned in passing how fortunate, how serendipitous their meeting had been. Just as casually, she revealed that she'd planned the whole thing. Right down to the lip biting.

At the time, he'd laughed, though he vaguely registered that now-familiar flutter of unease. But it didn't matter how they'd met. It was still love at first sight. Of the one-in-a-billion, once-in-a-lifetime variety.

'Hey, don't worry,' he says, standing behind her and giving her shoulders a tentative squeeze. Her muscles are rigid, and her mouth twitches at his touch. It's almost a flinch. 'We can make a Walmart run for the adaptor. It's not a big deal.'

'No, I know, I know.' Nikki shrugs off his hand, so discreetly he doesn't notice until he's left clutching at nothing but air. 'I just—' She drops onto the bed. Hair frames her face in a matted curtain; her eyes look straight ahead. Beyond him. As though they belong to a stranger, watching him. Watching them.

A few weeks after she was released from the hospital, Nikki reached for him in the dark. The first time in a long time. They kissed timidly, like high-schoolers under the scattered light of a prom disco ball. Clinical but intimate, uncomfortable but obligatory. The opposite of sex. And all the time, that faraway look in her eyes. The emptiness that stretched and yawned inside her, wrapping around the hollows of her bones and colouring her irises the pitch of black.

Still gripping the charger that won't charge where she's going, he finds he can't take it anymore. With a quiet mutter about getting them tea, he leaves. She and her haunted, hunted gaze. Looking at nothing, aching for nothing. A nothing that could've been something.

Nikki leaves for India at two-thirty in the morning. After she was released from the hospital, Neal's dads had stayed with them for two weeks, helping with the cooking, the cleaning. Everything they couldn't do anymore. But Nikki had spent hours and hundreds of dollars on long-distance phone calls to India. Finally, during a silent dinner two months later, she announced that she'd bought a ticket home. No discussion, no debate. She was going. He was welcome to join her, if he wanted.

Neal wakes up briefly, while she's struggling to lug her suitcase off the weighing scale. He makes coffee before he realizes she's already clutching a cup against her cheeks to warm her, a habit he used to find endearing.

'Hey, babe,' he says, and they both cringe at the endearment. 'Can I help with anything?'

She pushes the suitcase to the floor in defeat, tipping the scale over in the process. Blue digits glow upside-down in the darkness: 54 pounds.

'It's overweight.'

'Thank you,' she says. The suitcase has fallen on her toes, but she doesn't bother moving. They stare at it wordlessly.

After a pause, Neal squats and lifts the luggage off her feet, begins picking through its contents. The ornamented silverware set for Sheena Aunty. The new laptop for Nikki's nephew, the 'Amrikan' snacks for the niece. All absolute necessities. He holds up a video game console, about to ask if she *really* needs to gift this to that bratty cousin she never liked anyway, but the words die on his tongue when he looks up. She's not crying, but her lips are trembling, her eyes blinking rapidly. It's her trying-not-to-cry face, the one he knows too well by now.

They decide to screw it and just pay the fifty-dollar fee for excess baggage. He struggles to re-pack the suitcase, but it bulges out at odd angles, teetering unsteadily when he tries to balance it upright.

He offers to drive her to the airport, but she insists there's no need—it's a two-hour trip, and he has work later. The Uber driver they call is rated 4.1 stars; his picture is just the generic grey silhouette. Nikki stresses how she's *absolutely fine* with that. He makes her promise to call him while she's in the car, to keep texting him throughout the drive. She agrees.

'See you in two weeks?' he asks, after he's urged her to double check that she has her passport, ID, wallet, and boarding pass. Twice.

As though she's just remembered she's supposed to, she hugs him with one hand. 'Two weeks.'

In two weeks, his school semester will wind down, and he'll join her in India for a month. They'll come back together. They'll move on with their lives. That's the plan.

He forgets that he promised to stay up for her, and wakes up at 7:30 to three missed calls and four texts. The last one reads: *I'm alive, just so you know. Just boarded. Bye.*

She's back again.

Lisa, the pretty brunette with a lip ring and a keen eye for Chaucer, has stopped by during his office hours religiously for the past three weeks. Sometimes she comes with questions prepared; sometimes she just plops herself down in the seat across from him with easy familiarity. 'How are you doing, Professor Drew-Palmer?' she'll ask, and he'll pause, smile despite himself, and neglect to correct her that he's not a professor, not yet.

This time, they're looking at the Ellesmere manuscript. He has a photocopied folio on his desk, so she leans across the surface to get a better view, the V of her sweater plunging precariously low.

'Compare this illumination to the relatively poorly-done miniature of the monk,' Neal says, making a stalwart effort to keep his eyes on her violet contact lenses. 'That's what makes people think there may have been a second illustrator.'

'Wow,' she murmurs, looking up at him, still much too close. 'How fascinating.' The fricative 'f' sound hangs heavy in the air.

Neal clears his throat, pushes fogging glasses up his suddenly-sweaty nose. 'Yes, it is intriguing. Anyway, Ms Greene, I should get going, but, as always, it's been a pleasure.'

She stands up delicately, tugging at the skirt riding up her thighs. 'Thank you so much for making the time, Professor. I'll see you next week.'

When he's sure she's gone, Neal closes the heavy wooden door, slippery fingers fumbling with the doorknob. He lets out a long breath.

He hates Chaucer. He's always hated Chaucer. And here he is, flirting with undergrads over Chaucer's grave.

Grabbing the yellowing folio so roughly the page edge tears a little, he shoves it back in his desk. The bookcase behind him is filled with works by Tagore, Desai, Ghosh. Texts in Sanskrit and Hindi and Urdu. Mocking him in precise Times New Roman.

'So, let me get straight,' he remembers Nikki saying once, in her old singsong accent.

'Get *this* straight,' he'd corrected, tucking one of her dyed-brown locks behind the constellation of piercings studding her ear. They were sitting on a park bench, swaddled in the late afternoon. Their third date.

She smacked his hand away playfully, still in the phase where she found his nitpicking charming. 'Whatever. Get you straight, okay. You are Indian. You study Indian books. So why are you so…white?'

He hesitated for two cricket-chirps in the background.

This was the part where he always lost them. When he explained that, at the age of three, he'd been 'rescued' from a Calcutta orphanage by the Jasons, who always had the best of intentions. That his dads, the openly gay couple with the brown but very white son, had been so puzzled when Neal announced that he wasn't going to study law, like they'd discussed all his life, but South Asian literature and culture.

'But why?' Dad (Jason Drew) had asked, his crosshatch brow furrowed. 'Didn't we teach you enough about it growing up? We always encouraged you to speak Hindi and celebrate Diwali. It's nice that you want to get to know your roots, but what about a job?'

Always the voice of reason, Papa (Jason Palmer) hushed his partner with a subtle forearm squeeze. 'Neal, I think it's great,' he'd said, sitting beside his son in a gesture of solidarity.

'You know we will support you in anything you do. We're just wondering—why the change?'

Neal found that he couldn't explain it to them. Maybe he didn't fully understand it himself. Maybe it had to do with that peculiar tug he'd felt as a child, when white kids would ask him if he worshipped elephants and brown kids would ask him what his name meant in Hindi. Or with the strange knot that became an uninvited but permanent resident of his stomach after he turned the last page of Amit Chaudhuri's *Calcutta: Two Years in the City*. He didn't remember much of the backdrop of his earliest years, and the parts he did came in snippets, blurry and dreamlike: jasmine flowers woven in oily black braids, humid nights and velvet sunsets, street vendors waking him every morning with their rapid-fire sales pitches.

Maybe it had to do with his childhood determination to finish every jigsaw puzzle he ever started.

Nikki listened to him without interrupting, her dark eyes quiet and still. After he finished talking, she circled her arms around his neck, pressing her hot cheek against his stubble. They watched the afternoon light melt into soft gold. Not quite a velvet sunset, but not bad.

Not bad at all.

Later that night, after they'd followed through on the promise of the third date, Nikki turned to him in bed. 'You know, Neal means blue in Hindi,' she said. 'Blue-Skinned One, for Lord Shiva. You are a warrior god.'

He could barely make out her features in the dark, but he felt the puffs of her breath against his lips. He kissed her, hard.

❧

When Neal gets home that day, he's lost for a second. Swallowed up by the sheer emptiness that greets him.

He bumbles about the kitchen for a few minutes, squinting hard at rows of snacks, mixes and neatly-labelled spices lining the pantry. Finally, he gives in, heating up a frozen burrito forgotten for so long that it was encased in a solid block of ice.

He doesn't have to eat at the table, he realizes with an excited childlike jolt. Burrito in one hand, he wanders around the suddenly unfamiliar corridors of his home, aimlessly running his fingers across the tacky wallpaper they've been swearing to 'fix up' ever since they moved in. Almost of their own volition, his feet bring him to the room that's been shut with a vengeance for weeks. That he hasn't dared to enter since coming back from the hospital.

Hesitantly, half-expecting the ghost of his son to be hiding behind the nursery door, he steps in. No ghosts. Suraj didn't live long enough to learn to say 'boo'.

The nursery is silent. The shadowy images of elephants and giraffes, residents of the now-ominous safari landscape decorating the room, march sombrely across the walls.

He sets his laptop down on the futile changing table, sits cross-legged below it. The dust settles around him. The world is quiet here.

The hushed gravitas of the space focuses his mind, injects him with some sort of feeling, some sort of drive. For weeks, he has been numb. Partly of his own doing: he's been sneaking the pills prescribed to Nikki during their ill-advised session of couple's therapy.

'Symptoms of depression and anxiety are completely normal, given what you're going through,' the shrink had said soothingly, his involuntary eye-twitch incongruous with his tone. 'These won't cure the pain, but they'll help. Somewhat.'

Nikki hadn't touched the orange CVS containers Neal diligently picked up for her.

'I can stand a lot of things,' she'd told him. 'The pain, the loneliness. But I can't stand the nothingness. And don't you dare try to make me.'

He hadn't. He just hoped she didn't notice that he could. Stand the nothingness. Embrace it, even.

Above the crib, still stuffed with pillows and toys, Nikki had hand-made a mobile that dangled the initials SDP. Suraj Dillon-Palmer. They'd bickered over Suraj's last name for months. The surnames Drew-Palmer and Dillon didn't lend themselves to further hyphenation. They'd create a hybrid monster. They settled; Neal would lose half of his surname, but pass on the initials DP.

Hyphenation. What bullshit. Drew-Palmer. Dillon-Drew-Palmer. What next? If Suraj had lived, his children would have been burdened with four names, at the very least. Of course, these children would never exist, and probably for the better—what baby could bear the weight of such a cumbersome name? Patchwork names for patchwork worlds. No matter how well-intentioned, stitched-together identities can never become whole. He knows that better than most.

Neal suddenly remembers a line from his dissertation: 'The Indian-American is a paradox,' he'd written. 'Suspended between worlds, second-generation immigrants necessarily shoulder the burden of representation without the pride of ownership.'

Indian-American. Even more bullshit. Half Indian, half American: 50/50, stars and chakras equally represented.

They live somewhere along the hyphen. Him and Nikki. There's nowhere else they can go. And every day, they dance further and further away from each other. One day, they'll fall off the serif edge altogether, into their own separate words. Their own separate worlds. Indian and American.

The email hadn't caught him entirely off-guard. In a fit of empowerment last week, fuelled by the abrupt termination of Lisa's office visits and his revived ambition, he'd written to the English Department Chair to say that he was sick of teaching Chaucer. That he knew he was assigned to teach it again next semester, but he wouldn't. He couldn't. It wasn't what he trained in, it wasn't what he was passionate about. Take it or leave it. Take him or leave him.

So, the reticent *please come see me* message Dr Miller sent him in response didn't exactly come as a surprise. Seated outside her office, his hands are jittery. But he's calmer now, more rational. He rehearses his plea in his mind: *Please, Dr Miller. I've been going through a personal tragedy. I wasn't thinking straight. I hope you can look past this.*

'Good afternoon, Neal.'

Dr Miller's tone is soft, her features scrunched up sympathetically. He knows now that he's in real trouble. She leads him into her office, taking off her glasses to reveal a concerned frown.

'So, I understand that you're upset with the curriculum for next semester,' she says, knitting her fingers into chin-table. 'Tell me about it.'

Sweat, down the bridge of his glasses. 'The thing is, Dr Miller, I didn't mean what I said in that email,' he says. 'Yes, I've been feeling a little outside my comfort zone, but I understand that's a crucial part of my learning experience. It's just that you hired me for my postcolonial specialization...'

'I'm going to stop you right there, Neal,' she interrupts. 'Listen, you're a great instructor. You get stellar evaluations. But you're a postdoc and your contract is up next year. I know we've talked about renewing it in the past, but, in light of recent events, the Department is now reconsidering.'

His heart is beating fast, so fast.

'What? No, Dr Miller, I'm so sorry, I think there's been a misunderstanding—'

'No, Neal,' she says, and her voice is impossibly gentle. 'I'm afraid we understand each other perfectly.'

He walks home in the rain. He'd been in the mood for a brisk walk that morning. Foolish, naïve Morning Neal. Who wasn't yet aware that he'd blown his chances in academia. In life. Shoulders shivering, teeth chattering, unsure of the origin of the wetness on his cheeks, he runs into the first door he sees.

The scene unfolds in slow motion.

A waiter comes up to him, smacking gum loudly before asking, 'How many, sir?'

He tries to speak, but words don't come out. His throat is raw. He holds up his index finger.

The waiter guides him to a corner seat, away from the happy families dominating the center of the dessert cafe. It's not the same seat. They've redecorated since the last time he was here. The chairs were plastic then, he thinks, but he might be remembering wrong.

It's close enough. To where he sat that day. Across from Nikki, her luminous eyes red and bloodshot. Their seventh date. They were still in the exploring stage: dessert cafes and art galleries and bungee-jumping. He wasn't sure how to react to her emotions, so he reached across the kitschy cushioned table, awkwardly clasping his hand over her tightly-curled fist.

She'd just heard that her application for the EB-1 green card had been rejected. The Extraordinary Ability green card. Deemed categorically mediocre by no less an authority than the US government, she had no choice but to return to India when her student visa expired. In two months.

He'd listened to her mutely, helplessly. There was a burning in his chest. He squeezed her hand tighter, and to his surprise, she opened her palm and laced her fingers through his. She squeezed back.The touch sent shivers through his body.

'Marry me,' he blurted out, so recklessly he surprised even himself. 'Marry me, and all of this goes away.'

She was stunned into silence. Lips vibrating, eyes blinking rapidly. Her trying-not-to-cry face, though he didn't know it back then.

The waiter seemed even more shocked than the two of them. Quickly conferring with his colleagues, he returned to their table with a giant chocolate cupcake and a huge smile plastered on his face.

'Congratulations to the happy couple!' he exclaimed, setting the plate down in front of Nikki.

She took one look at it and burst into tears.

Now, Neal pretends to wipe raindrops from his face.

This time, the journey to the airport is uneventful. He packs his suitcase carefully, weighing it even though he knows his meagre belongings don't amount to fifty pounds. He drinks his coffee, brushes his teeth, eats his granola bar. In silence. In the dark. When the Uber driver pulls up, he says, 'I'll give you five stars if you don't talk to me.'

The driver, a measly 4.3'er, does not complain.

Neal is mildly surprised, as always, when he's pulled aside by the TSA for a random pat-down. Sometimes, he forgets his insides don't match his outsides. They don't find anything, and he boards the plane. Even before takeoff, he closes his eyes.

'Excuse me, sir?'

The woman in the middle seat. Oversized sunglasses perch atop her bleached-blonde head; long nails clack incessantly at her phone screen.

He thinks maybe if he keeps up the pretense of sleep, she'll leave him alone. No. The woman is dogged. She clears her throat, again and again, until he snaps his eyes open and snarls, 'What?'

She's visibly taken aback. 'I'm sorry to disturb you,' she says. 'I was just hoping you could tell me a little bit about India. It's my first time there, you see.'

He would have rolled his eyes if he hadn't anticipated the question. 'It's my first time too, ma'am.'

She responds before he has a chance to feign sleep again. 'Oh! I didn't realize. So sorry, I just assumed.'

'Yeah, you guys do that a lot, don't you? Assume?' She has his attention now, just like she wanted.

Uncomfortably, she looks down, scraping her turquoise fake nails against each other. 'I'm so sorry, I didn't mean to offend you. I just got divorced, and I'm doing the India thing to... you know. Find myself.'

He scoffs, but something inside him loosens a little bit. His spine, steely with tension upon attack, relaxes against the sparsely-padded seat. 'Yeah, lady, I'm not really the one to ask about that *Eat, Pray, Love* shit. My wife lost her baby, so I'm going there to spend time with her family. But I haven't been back to India since my dads rescued me from an orphanage there when I was three.'

He's so sure he's horrified her into silence that he doesn't bother looking over for a response. He's stumped when he hears a feeble voice snaking into the silence.

'Wow, I'm sorry. That sounds really hard. But things have a way of working out for the better, you'll see. Maybe you'll be happier now.'

This time, he rolls his eyes openly. Exaggeratedly. She gets the message and thumbs through the SkyMall magazine for the rest of the flight. He goes back to fake-sleeping. Somewhere between closing his eyes and dreaming, though, her clichés clang in his brain.

Maybe you'll be happier now.

He's not sure what he expected from this visit. A homecoming, maybe. Or a lack thereof.

But not this. The smell of dung greets him the second he steps off the plane. Geckos stare at him from the floor, from the wall, from the ceiling. Sneakers and chappals alike kick up dust clouds that hang, petrified, in the heavy air.

Everything feels familiar-but-strange. Like reconstructing memories by staring at old photographs for too long. Like checking the time on a watch that's stopped.

'Arrey, bhaisaab!' Nikki's brother, Mukesh, yells when he sees him. He's holding up a sign with both hands. *Neel From U.S.A*, it says. He looks like Nikki—same dark eyes, same thick hair and uneven teeth. On him, it doesn't work.

It's the first time he's meeting Mukesh. None of Nikki's family could make it to the rushed wedding. Mukesh chatters endlessly, strings of questions he leaves Neal no space to answer. *How is Amrika? How is the weather there? Must be chilly, nah? Here, it never snows. I wish I could see snow. Do you have snow there now?*

Neal's timing couldn't be better, Mukesh informs him. Their distant cousin, Priya—Mukesh isn't even sure of the exact relation—is getting engaged tomorrow. The festivities have started at home. It'll be a great introduction to the family, he promises. To India.

The car turns in the gate of the house—a palace, more accurately. Nikki had mentioned she was from a well-off family, but Neal could never have imagined this—he's immediately lost in a sea of well-meaning arms and bosoms—in kisses, pinches, exclamations over how handsome he is, so much handsomer than the pictures. Riya Aunty, Akash Uncle, Chitra Didi, Rohan Bhai. The list goes on. There's so many of them that it takes him a good ten minutes to find Nikki.

They lock eyes over the mass of saris and bindis and dhotis, but she immediately looks away, down at the floor. Demurely. She's standing by the staircase, dressed in a traditional cotton sari, a shy smile fluttering on her lips. The blushing Indian bride she never got a chance to be. He leans in to kiss her, but her meaningful glare tells him that's a bad idea. He settles for holding her hand instead, relishing the roughness of her palms, the sting of her bangles cutting into his wrist.

He's fed. A lot. An aunty keeps heaping his plate with biryani, just as he struggles through the last bite. He finally has to tell her to stop; he's chided for being 'so diet-y—such an Amrikan!'

After what feels like hours—his perception of time has blurred over the course of the twenty-two hour journey—Nikki leads him up to a room on the third level of the house. Pink, airy, with an ornately-carved four-poster bed complete with billowing canopy. Her cheeks are flushed, and he notices that she's wearing lipstick within the lines.

He reaches for her, but she pushes him away. 'Not here!' she gasps, almost giggling. 'My family will know.'

Her family. Her world.

They don't talk. They have a lot to say, but no way to say it. They lie on opposite sides of that enormous bed, so wide that they need separate blankets. Her back is curved away from him, and he can tell by the soft rise-and-fall of her silhouette that she's asleep. Soundly. For once.

Maybe you'll be happier now.

He lies awake. The wall opposite the foot of the bed is covered with mirrors, panes upon panes of mirrors. Their glassy doppelgangers are fractured, splintered into a thousand glittering shards. Through the looking glass, even Nikki's peaceful sleep-smile seems sinister. He shifts, moulding his reflection into the dark cleft between mirrors. He stares at the pink three-pronged ceiling fan, futilely circulating hot air. A gecko, camouflaged pink but not quite well enough, stares back at him.

Tara

You are born the day your grandmother dies, a Friday, with your father's coarse curls, your mother's hard eyes, and memories of monsoons you have never seen. They pick you apart from the beginning, each staking their claims: your nose, bent like your achacha's (he went to jail two years ago—molestation—but we don't talk about that). Your lips, pink and right and almost white: your grandmother's, without a doubt. Your family spans three continents, four time-zones, five surnames. They unite, for the first time, on your face. Your blood curdles with history.

Your name was supposed to be Susan, after your grandmother, Susamma. Susan, soft and simple. But when you are born on that doomed day, smiling, your mother reconsiders. You are not her, little naadan Rincy, or your grandmother. You are not soft and simple. Your mother makes a promise, then, that she doesn't yet know she can't keep: she will raise her baby to be a westerner, she vows. A go-getter, a winner. She can do anything; *you* can do anything. So, despite your father's protests, your mother names you Nivedita: *offered to God*. A Hindu name. A majestic name, she thinks. A name that curls, diaphanous, on the tongue.

As a baby, you wear the name well, your mother tells you later, as if you recognized the privilege. Just days old, you refuse to smile when toothless uncles call you pretty. Those strange, damp days in England, back when everything was new, your mother gleans small warmth from holding you, from dressing you in these outlandish costumes—jeans for a baby, whoever heard of such a thing?—from whispering your name, over and over, *Nivedita*, like a prayer.

You belong to everyone and no one, to everywhere and nowhere. Lost in the gridlock, caught between continents, you don't know how to pronounce your name. You don't know if you want to learn.

If you have a daughter, you will name her Tara. An easy name. A name to appease the East and the West. Rooted in India—Tara for star, Tara for precious star, Tara for my star—but palatable for Western tongues. Tara is a name that won't cause teachers to stumble and stutter during roll call. It's a name that will help your daughter introduce herself confidently, to speak out in class unhesitatingly, to shake an interviewer's hand and not worry about correcting his pronunciation. She will be able to hear her name in a way you have not: her friends will say it to her face instead of avoiding it, her partner will whisper it to her in between kisses, her professors won't hesitate to call on it during discussions.

Tara. It's a cop-out name.

Acknowledgements

Six of the stories in *The Juvenile Immigrant* were first published in different forms across various outlets: 'Monsoon' in *Teen Ink* (2014) and in *Litro Magazine* (2016) as 'Desi Girl'; 'It Dreamt Itself Away' in *Teen Ink* (2014) as 'Dreams and Lies'; 'Naale' in *Teen Ink* (2014); 'Guide to Bharatanatyam' in *Paper Darts* (2017) as a fiction piece and in *World Literature Today* (2019) as a poem; 'Spellbound' in *World Literature Today* (2019); and 'Kathakali' in *Nimrod International Journal of Prose and Poetry* (2018) as a poem and in Spider Road Press (2017) as a flash fiction piece.

I would also like to express my gratitude to the team at Speaking Tiger—in particular, to my editor, Kartikeya Jain, for his precise and thoughtful work on this collection, and to Renuka Chatterjee, for taking a chance on my manuscript.

Finally, thank you, always, to my family. You are the reason I can afford to be brave.

BODY AND BLOOD
STORIES ON BREAKING THE TEN COMMANDMENTS

Urmilla Deshpande

Each story in this first-of-its-kind collection takes you into a realm where people are prompted by love, desire, jealousy, hatred and, at times, a strange compassion, to throw out the old, conventional rules, and make their own. The title story, 'Body and Blood', is a macabre revelation of how far one can go when one loves someone before all others, even God; in 'Honour. Or Not', a young girl abused by her father since the age of thirteen finds a shockingly unexpected way of 'honouring' him when he dies.

In a lighter vein, the protagonist in 'Sunday Snow Job' asserts that working girls have to work, even on the Holy Sabbath, while Gomes in 'Heart of Gold' finds it is possible to covet your neighbour's wife and get rich too. 'Wakulla' raises the question: can stealing be an act of compassion, and not a sin? In 'Fall', Srinivas discovers that one can make love to one's best friend's wife without actually committing adultery. And coveting your neighbour's goods is fine—as long as they are the right ones, as 'Elegy in a Churchyard', the tenth story in this rivetting collection, teaches us.

Written with panache and by turns erotic, tongue-in-cheek and shocking, this is a collection of noir and black humour at its best.

SUNITA DE SOUZA GOES TO SYDNEY
AND OTHER STORIES

Roanna Gonsalves

Winner of the Multicultural NSW Award 2018

'*Sunita De Souza Goes to Sydney* comprises 16 stories which display Gonsalves's immense range and sensitivity in negotiating the uneven contours of human relationships.... Her felicity with language is one of the major strengths of the book.... This is a reassuring debut of a very compassionate new voice.'—*Biblio*

A woman who can't swim wades into a suburban pool. An Indian family sits down to an Australian Christmas dinner. A single mother's offer to coach her son's football team leads to an unexpected encounter, and a wife refuses to let her husband look at her phone.

Roanna Gonsalves' short stories unearth the aspirations, ambivalence and guilt laced through the lives of twenty-first century Indian immigrants to Australia, steering through clashes of cultures, trials of faith, and squalls of racism. Sometimes heartwrenching, sometimes playful, they cut to the truth of what it means to be a modern outsider. Since its publication, Sunita De Souza Goes to Sydney has quickly found a place on a number of lists of must-read books, and has been praised by critics for its playfulness with language, its boldness and its fresh voice.